THE ADVENTURES OF JOHNNY, LUKE, AND MICHAEL

Includes
Joey Spaghetti and the Baxter Bunch
Stormy Weathers
The Skateboard King
The Cruise Caper

John F. Lawson DDS

Contents

Acknowledgements

I would like to thank Bonnie Pickett for her generosity and talents. Your gift to me made my dream possible.

Thanks to Meggie and Mo for your support and love.

Thanks to Johnny, Michael, and Luke for being the special kind of friends that inspired me.

Joey Spaghetti and the Baxter Bunch

To Johnny - The best friend I've ever had

CHAPTER ONE

"Hey, we're up here," Johnny said to Luke as he stuck his head out of the window. His head barely fit through the sliding window on the front of the fort. It was where the boys spent most of their time when they weren't playing some sort of sport.

"Password?" Michael asked as he tried to stick his head out too.

"You two look pretty funny up there!" Luke said, chuckling. "Like a two-headed monster or something!"

"Well, it doesn't matter and don't try to get out of saying the password!" said Michael. This was funny to Johnny and Luke as Michael could never seem to remember the passwords anyway. The boys would change them each week to keep out trespassers. Not that anyone tried to get in the fort, but you can't have a club without a password.

"I know the password, Michael," said Luke. "Johnny told me yesterday. Why do we have one anyway? Megan can come in here whenever she wants!"

Megan was Johnny's older sister. Even though he tried to convince his mom she shouldn't be allowed to come in the fort, his mom didn't agree.

"Password?" Michael asked again.

Luke finally relented and yelled out, "Double play!"

"OK, you can enter," Johnny said, and he opened the door on the bottom of the fort.

None of the boys knew how long they had been friends, but as far as they could remember they'd been best friends. If two of them were together, the third one was surely on his way to meet them. It was a rare thing to see them when they weren't together. Luke was the shortest of the three, but not by much. Johnny was maybe an inch or so taller, but Michael towered over the both of them. That wasn't surprising as Michael had turned eleven already. Johnny and Luke's birthdays hadn't even come up yet. The three boys all had blonde hair, but Michael was the only one with curly hair. As a matter of fact, it was impossible to tell the difference between Johnny and Luke from the back.

"What took you so long anyway?" Johnny asked.

"I'll show you. Send down the bucket, Johnny," Luke said. "My mom made us some cookies."

"Chocolate chip?" Johnny questioned as he crossed both his fingers. "I hope so. Your mom makes the best cookies!"

"Of course!" Luke said proudly. "She sent some milk too. Don't drink it all this time, Michael." Michael had the habit of eating most of the food and drinking all of the milk. The other two boys drank milk only when they were forced, but Michael could drink a gallon by himself. With cookies, however, milk was everyone's favorite.

Johnny lowered the bucket with the rope and pulley system that his dad and grandpa designed when they made the fort. It was the coolest fort in all of Mapleville and all the boys knew it. The fort was a large square built on top of four large wooden posts. It had a triangular roof with green shingles and it was painted a light brown on the outside. Johnny's dad had decided to build it next to an old oak tree and it was tucked neatly between two of the largest branches. You might not think it was the coolest fort by looking at it from the outside, but the inside was what the boys liked.

Before Johnny's dad and grandpa had put up the outside walls of the fort, they set up a bunk bed inside. The bottom bunk was a double bed that could be made into a couch and the top was a single bed. It was perfect for sleepovers for the three of them. They played rock, paper, scissors to determine who got to sleep on the top bunk. The top was the best because it had the best view of the old television that Mr. Beardsley down the street had given them when he came to watch the building of the fort.

Johnny's grandpa had made shelves on the wall for the television and the DVD player that he bought for the boys.

Johnny raised the bucket up carefully and pulled it inside the fort. As soon as he removed the cookies and milk, Luke took the last step onto the floor of the clubhouse.

"What you guys watching?" Luke asked without looking at the television.

"Bond movie," Johnny said. "What else? We always watch Bond movies."

The whole set of Bond movies was a permanent fixture in the fort. On rainy days they might watch two or three of them in a row. Only, of course, if they had enough food.

Johnny stood up right then and made a gun out of his right index finger and thumb. He grabbed his right wrist with his left hand and shouted, "Name is Lawson, Johnny Lawson." He tried to make the accent like the real James Bond did in his movies.

All three boys started humming the theme song to the movies and ended it by shooting each other and falling to the floor as they had done hundreds of times. It usually ended up with fits of laughter until they started watching the movie again. This time was no different.

Fifteen minutes later, two dozen cookies had been devoured and all the milk was gone. Michael ate the most as usual, but there were plenty so Johnny and Luke didn't mind. Johnny got up and turned off the television. He stood in front of the set with a serious look on his face.

CHAPTER TWO

"Guys, we have a problem. Tomorrow Mrs. G will be giving us a topic for our group project," he stated.

Mrs. Greenfield was their fifth grade teacher. She was probably the nicest fifth grade teacher on the planet, but she was hard. If anyone had a problem in her class, she would do anything to help them understand the lesson. She had a special way of connecting to her students and could tell the most captivating stories. She didn't even mind being called Mrs. G, and they thought that was cool. The boys thought that she had been teaching for a hundred years, but of course that couldn't be true.

"I have a plan, but we are going to have to be quick about it," Johnny said with determination. "One of us will have to be asked to pull the topics from the hat. It's the only chance we will have."

"We have to get Lebron James!" Michael said as he looked at the other two. "I don't want to do something dumb again. Last time I was grouped with David and Mary and we had Laura Ingalls Wilder."

"Yuck!" Luke exclaimed. "That's worse than having to sit by Mary Beth McDermott!"

Luke had been seated by Mary Beth for two months and she was always trying to kiss him. He found the best way to avoid her was to turn his desk almost sideways away from her.

"I still can't believe you got Mrs. G to put us in the same group," Michael said. "How did you do it?"

Johnny plopped back down on the bed and leaned back on the pillow with his hands behind his head. "I went up to her this morning and begged her to put us together. I told her that we have never been together. I'm ingenious. Aren't I?" he said.

Luke and Michael immediately dove on top of him and pretended to pound him with their fists. They all laughed and wrestled for a couple of minutes before they tired.

Johnny started again. "She actually said no at first, but I begged her over and over. I promised her that we would do a great job."

The truth was that Mrs. Greenfield sometimes had to separate the boys in class because they would wind up talking about their favorite sport, which usually changed to the one that they were playing at the time.

"So, if all three of us volunteer really quickly to pick the topics from the hat, then maybe we can peek and pick the one we want," Johnny pleaded.

Luke jumped in. "Lebron James! Lebron James! It would be really easy. I have two books about him already. Michael has three!"

"My dad got me his rookie card too. Maybe we will get extra credit for showing it to everyone!" Johnny exclaimed.

"I sure hope so, but what if we get someone else?" Michael said, looking depressed. "We probably will get one of the topics the girls picked anyway."

Every month Mrs. Greenfield would ask the class for some topics and she would call on ten or so children for ideas. Today, there were many different topics, from sports figures to politicians to villains. Michael suggested Lebron James because this was basketball season. Kelsey, who did nothing but skate, picked Michelle Kwan. Cole could only think of George Bush because he raised his hand without thinking, so the first person that came to his mind was the president. Joey Spinelli picked the Baxter Bunch, a gang from the 1800s. In addition, there were a few entertainers and even Mickey Mouse.

Mrs. G didn't really mind what topics were picked because she wanted the kids to work together on gathering information and then presenting a speech to the class. All three of the children in each group had to speak so she knew that everyone knew the subject.

"Well if we don't get Lebron, then I hope we get Mickey Mouse!" Luke laughed. "My brother, sister, and I still have our mouse ears from our Disney trip and the three of us could wear them!"

The boys looked at each other oddly and decided without even saying anything that wearing mouse ears was out of the question.

"Let's just stick to the plan and raise our hands first so we can pick Lebron!" Johnny said.

Luke jumped in and said, "What time is your game tonight anyway?"

"It's 6:30 p.m. and we play Sacred Heart for the championship. They are so tall!" Michael said.

"And they're quick!" Johnny added.

Luke had decided not to play basketball this year even though they played endless hours on Johnny's driveway. If you were looking for the boys, they could easily be found playing horse or pretending to make the last second three-point shot to win the NBA championship.

"I wish I was playing with you guys. I don't know what I was thinking when I decided to sit out," said Luke. "I'll be there cheering for you guys though."

"Hey, you still have the pickle ball finals tomorrow in gym class," Johnny added trying to make Luke feel better. "You'll beat Danny R easy for sure."

Danny R stood for Danny Rodriquez because there was a Danny Johnson in the class too.

"I barely beat Danny J yesterday," Luke said. "The score was 7 to 5 in a close game."

"Don't you think it's odd that all the Dannys in the class are good at pickle ball? I do," Michael added.

Luke had won the pickle ball tournament for his grade for the past three years, but now that Danny R had moved to town he wasn't so sure. Danny was from Texas where the weather is nicer and they could play outside all year long.

"Who invented pickle ball anyway?" Johnny asked. "A paddle and wiffle ball played on a mini-tennis court. It just seems so odd."

"It is a bit funny," Michael added. "Doesn't matter Luke, because you're gonna whip Danny R all the way to Texas!"

With that the boys clenched their right hands into fists and touched them together. "Knuckles!" they exclaimed. The touching of knuckles was the unofficial secret handshake of the clubhouse.

CHAPTER THREE

The Holy Spirit Jaguars' fifth grade basketball team was undefeated this year, but so was the Sacred Heart team. Johnny and Michael's team, the Jaguars, relied on hustle and speed. Sacred Heart had some quick players, but those boys were known mostly for their height. David Anderson, or "The Stork" as most of the boys called him, was almost six feet tall. His father and older brothers were even taller, so David would probably even grow more. Some of the kids even thought he grew between games. It would be tough to beat the Stork and his tall teammates.

Luke was in the stands with his dad sitting next to Johnny's and Michael's dads. The excitement was building in the gym for the opening tip off. There were ten boys on the Jaguars, so the coach split them into two squads. The blue squad would start and the red squad would come in next. Occasionally the coach would mix players from both squads because the best players were not on the same team, and he wanted to have balance on both blue and red. Johnny played for the blue side and got to start the game.

Billy Thomas, the tallest kid on the team, got to take the tip for Holy Spirit but everyone knew the Stork would get the ball and not even have to jump.

"Go Jaguars!" Luke shouted from the stands. "Go Johnny! Go Michael!" He had no problem screaming encouragement for his buddies.

The tip off, of course, went to Sacred Heart, and the game was underway. Baskets seemed to fall much easier for the Sacred Heart team and the Stork got just about every rebound. Coach Donaker was pacing up and down the sidelines as his team was having difficulty making plays against the taller team.

Johnny was the fastest boy on his team and could move left and right with ease. Still, the blue team was having difficulty getting the ball to the basket after he got the ball to their side of the court.

"Settle down you guys!" Coach yelled from the bench. "Play your game."

Before long the Stork and his team mates were up 10 to 6 and seemed to be in control of the game. Coach then took out the blue squad and gave the red squad a chance at the towering Sacred Heart boys.

"It's hard to shoot over them," Johnny wheezed. "They are too tall. We are all a bunch of nervous wrecks out there."

Coach Donaker listened but didn't say anything. He knew that Johnny was probably right, but for now he would watch the red squad and hope that things would turn around.

Now it was Michael's turn. Michael was the best hustler on the whole team and he was strong as well.

His shot was kind of funny as he brought the ball way down to his right side at the beginning. As weird as it was, however, he had the most points on the team and made most of his shots.

Danny J was dribbling the ball for the red squad and barely got it down to Michael, who faked left and then drove to the right and was fouled by the Stork.

Michael went to the free throw line and made both shots for the struggling Jaguars.

"We'll take them anyway we can get them!" exclaimed Coach Donaker. Coach sounded a little desperate, but he sounded like that most of the time they played, even when they were up by twenty points.

By halftime the treelike boys of Sacred Heart had a ten point lead. Things were not going well. The Jaguars huddled around the coach as he took out his clipboard and diagrammed some plays.

Joey Spinelli lumbered up the bleachers and sat down next to Luke. Joey had the nickname Joey Spaghetti because it seemed like he always had spaghetti sauce on his shirt. Joey didn't mind the nickname; actually, he was proud of it. He was the largest boy in his class by at least fifty pounds. That made perfect sense because Joey was always eating.

"Want some popcorn, Luke?" Joey asked. "I got a large bag so I could share. It's buttered too!"

"You always get a large bag, Joey!" Luke chuckled. "No thanks though. I'm too nervous, anyway." Luke smiled as he saw the butter all over Joey's chin.

"What's the deal today? The guys can't seem to score," Joey Spaghetti mumbled, his mouth was full of popcorn.

"I think the coach is going to have to play his best players all on one side soon. Or else we'll lose for sure!" Luke said.

"I think I'd better run down to my dad's hardware store and get some ladders for our team. That's the only way they are going to shoot over the Stork!" shouted Joey.

"Well, you had better hurry," said Luke. "We only have one half left."

Luke chuckled to himself. He knew that Joey Spaghetti couldn't hurry and do anything. At his size, speed didn't come in any shape or form.

The second half started about the same as the first. Johnny's squad was holding the Sacred Heart lead to ten. They just couldn't seem to get any closer.

Coach sent in the red squad and Michael was hustling and grabbing every loose ball he could. With less than two minutes left to go, the Stork and his team were leading the Holy Spirit Jaguars 38 to 30.

Michael grabbed another rebound and the coach called time out.

"Johnny, go in for Danny J and Michael you stay in the game!" Coach yelled. "We are going to pressure the dribbler everywhere on the court."

Johnny smiled. He rarely got to play alongside Michael. Michael grinned back.

"Johnny, I want you to run the fast break for the rest of the game. Go as quick as you can up the court," Coach said.

Johnny nodded while he took a drink from his water bottle. "I will, Coach."

The game started up again and Johnny brought the ball quickly up the court. He moved the ball to Michael's side of the court and made a bounce pass as Michael broke for the basket. The Stork never saw it coming, and Michael made an easy layup for two more points.

The Sacred Heart team didn't see the pressure coming and made a bad pass that Johnny intercepted easily. He bounced the ball off the glass for another layup and another two points.

This time the Stork wasn't going to be fooled as easily; he decided to throw the ball in himself. Sacred Heart moved the ball to the other half of the court quickly. One of the guards took a shot, and it bounced hard off the rim and flew out of the reach of the Stork underneath the basket. Michael grabbed the ball and passed it to Johnny.

Johnny began to fly up the court. He went left and right and then left and then right again. His friends had coined his move "The Weave." The boy guarding him was running backwards and trying to keep up when he tripped over his own two feet!

Johnny took advantage of the mistake and started again to his right for another easy layup.

Immediately the other coach called time out. The score was 38 to 36 with the Jaguars trailing by just two points with thirty-one seconds left to go.

"We are going to keep putting pressure on the dribblers," Coach Donaker explained. "Try not to foul unless you have no other choice. I want you to get the ball back as quick as you can and then we can try and tie the game."

As the clock started again, the Sacred Heart team brought the ball down the court and began to pass the ball around. Precious seconds were ticking away and the Jaguars couldn't seem to get the ball back.

"Fire up Johnny! Steal the ball!" screamed Luke.

Johnny heard Luke up in the stands and he got a determined look in his eye.

"Ten – Nine – Eight – Seven," Luke and others yelled from the stands.

As the Sacred Heart player leaned to the left to pass to the Stork, Johnny dove to intercept the ball. He landed on the ground as he knocked the ball down the court. Johnny struggled to his feet and tried to grab the ball as it was heading out of bounds.

"Five – Four – Hurry, Johnny!" Luke yelled.

Michael was on the other side of the court at the half way line. He yelled "Johnny, over here!"

Johnny grabbed the ball and threw it backwards over his head towards Michael while jumping out of bounds. Johnny landed right on top of the scorer's table.

Michael leaped into the air and grabbed the ball.

"Shoot, Michael, shoot!" Coach screamed, waving his hands and jumping up and down.

Michael took the ball and dropped his arms way down on the side and let ball fly just before the time expired on the clock. It seemed that the ball was flying in slow motion as it made its way toward the basket. Johnny was standing on the scorer's table now, watching the ball. The ball bounced on the front of the rim and flew straight up ten feet into the air. Then it came down to swish the net.

"Three-pointer! Three-pointer!" Johnny screamed as he jumped from the table.

Johnny ran over to Michael along with the rest of the team. Everyone was congratulating Michael for his great shot. The scoreboard read 39 to 38 in favor of the Holy Spirit Jaguars.

"That shot was awesome, Michael! Just like we practiced at home!" Johnny said. "That was the coolest shot ever!"

"Your steal made it possible, you know," Michael said as he made a knuckle. Luke came running up and made a knuckle too.

"Knuckles!" the three boys yelled.

Johnny's dad walked up and congratulated them on a great game. Michael's dad was smiling so big you could see every one of his teeth. It wasn't a surprise that he offered to buy everyone ice cream.

"Can I come too?" asked Joey Spaghetti.

Michael's dad's agreed and they all headed out the door.

"I'm not sure if my dad has enough money to fill up Joey," said Michael.

The three boys laughed all the way to the ice cream shop.

CHAPTER FOUR

School was busy as usual, and the children were busy with their papers. Luke thought the day was going well since Mary Beth McDermott hadn't tried to kiss him even once. He was excited about gym class and the chance to play for the pickle ball title.

Mrs. Greenfield stood and asked the students to put away their papers. Johnny looked over at Michael and Luke and gave them a wink. He motioned a little with his arm to get them ready to raise their hands quickly.

"Since it is Andrea's birthday today, I am going to ask her to come up and draw the names out of the hat for your monthly topics. Once you have your topic, your group can begin to gather information for your speech," Mrs. Greenfield said. "And remember, everyone has to participate."

Johnny sunk his head onto his desk. "We are doomed," he whispered across the aisle to Michael.

Michael nodded and began to cross his fingers and toes and legs too. "Lebron James. Lebron James," he muttered under his breath.

The first group to go was made up of the Dannys and Suzie, the cutest girl in all the school. Andrea dug her hand into the hat and read the name on the piece of paper.

"The first group's topic is Mickey Mouse," she laughed.

Luke let out a sigh of relief and tilted his head to the side as he looked at Johnny. He pretended to wipe sweat off his forehead and fling it away. "Whew," he mouthed.

Five other groups had gone and Lebron's name was still in the hat!

The second to last group to go was Joey Spaghetti, Billy Thomas, and Mary Beth McDermott. Joey had his eyes closed, wishing for something. Johnny was sure it was for Lebron James, the best basketball player in the NBA.

Andrea reached into the hat and stated clearly, "The next topic is Lebron James!"

With that, Johnny, Luke, Michael, and Joey Spaghetti let out a simultaneous "Uggghhhh."

The entire class started laughing and Mrs. Greenfield had to get everyone to settle down to finish the topics.

"The last group is Michael, Johnny, and Luke. Andrea, please draw a name out of the hat," Mrs. Greenfield said.

"The final topic is the Baxter Bunch." She snickered. "Thank you for letting me pick the names, Mrs. G."

Johnny glanced over toward Luke and noticed that Joey Spaghetti looked like he was about to cry.

CHAPTER FIVE

Everyone was in the gym, sitting on the bleachers and on the floor near the walls. The pickle ball finals were completed for the first four grades. Luke was getting ready to go when Johnny and Michael motioned him over to where they were sitting.

"Remember, you can beat him easy," said Johnny. "Use that rocket shot of yours that you use on me."

"No sweat," said Michael. "Johnny's right. Use that rocket shot. Good luck!"

Mr. Krowley, the gym teacher, introduced the next two finalists and motioned them to begin to play. Danny R served first and they began to hit the ball back and forth across the net. The first point was a grueling one that lasted as long as any pickle ball point in the history of the tournament. Then Danny R hit the ball to the corner just out of the reach of Luke for the first point.

Joey Spaghetti moved over Suzie and Danny J to get to Michael and Johnny. At one point Danny thought that Joey might fall backwards and sit on him, so he shoved him back upright. Joey finally made it down the bleachers next to Johnny.

"Johnny, we have to talk," said Joey. "I really wanted to get the Baxter Bunch."

"C'mon Luke, you can do it!" Johnny yelled at the top of his lungs. "Hit it to his left!"

"Really, Johnny. I want to do my report on the Baxter Bunch," pleaded Joey. "That's why I suggested it for a topic."

"Way to go, Luke," Johnny screamed as Luke got his first point. The score was now 2 to 1 in favor of Danny R.

"Please Johnny, trade with me, please? I know nothing about Lebron James. I can't stand the NBA," said Joey.

Johnny finally turned in the direction of Joey Spaghetti. His mouth was open and his eyes were wide with amazement. "Can't stand the NBA? What are you – crazy? I can't believe you even said that," he cried out. "Hey Michael, did you hear that?"

"Well, he would know who Lebron James was if he was made out of food!" Michael laughed. "I bet he would make a great candy bar! It would be huge too. I bet they would name it the King James bar. That's Lebron's nickname, Joey, but you probably wouldn't know that."

"We would love to switch with you, but Mrs. G would never let us," Johnny explained. "That's her rule and she's never let anyone switch before."

Just then the ball came flying up into the bleachers and flew right by Joey's nose. It missed by a hair and Joey never even saw it.

"Please Johnny, can't you just try and ask her to trade," Joey pleaded.

"Ok already. I'll try. Just let me watch the game." Johnny looked over at Michael and shrugged his shoulders.

The game had progressed and now it was 6 to 5 in favor of Luke. It was long and intense and Luke was getting tired. Hopefully one more point for him and it would be over. He put his hands on his knees and looked up in the stands at Michael and Johnny with a tired expression.

Johnny made a fist and Michael made one too. They touched them together and mouthed "rocket shot" at the same time. Luke nodded back.

Luke served the ball and the last point began. The two boys ran back and forth and left and right. Luke made a great shot to the left and Danny R got to it just in time to make a return. The ball flew a little too high across the net, and Luke knew this was his chance. Luke got his feet ready and raised his paddle high in the air. He swung as hard as he could and connected mightily with the ball. The little ball went flying directly at Danny R's head, and before he had time to react it glanced off the top of his noggin. It went flying backwards and landed way out of bounds.

Danny R knew he had lost and reached over the net to shake Luke's hand.

"Great game, Luke. What do you call that shot anyway?" he asked?

"Rocket shot!" Johnny and Michael yelled as they ran up to Luke. Michael continued to talk with Luke while Johnny walked over to Mrs. G, who was standing in the corner of the gym.

Luke received his trophy from Mr. Krowley and then sat down next to Michael back in the stands.

"Where's Johnny?" he asked Michael. Michael pointed in Mrs. G's direction as she was emphatically shaking her head no.

"I guess we are stuck with the Baxter Bunch," said Michael, "and Joey is gonna have to learn about the best basketball player in the whole world."

CHAPTER SIX

"Johnny, you got a phone call from that spaghetti guy," said Megan. She got home earlier than her brother because she got a ride home. Johnny could have too, but he wanted to ride the bus with Michael and Luke.

He threw his backpack on the table and opened the fridge while he looked for a snack.

"Michael called and said he and Luke would be right over," she added. "Didn't you get off the bus with them a minute ago?"

"Yeah, so what?" Johnny quipped.

"Couldn't they have told you on the bus? I mean, that they would be right over?" she asked, perturbed.

"I suppose, but who cares anyway?" Johnny said.

"What if I missed a call? My friends could have been trying to call you know." Megan was agitated.

"You mean Kevin might have been trying to call, right?" Johnny snickered.

"Mom!" Megan yelled as she stormed out of the room.

The back door opened and Michael and Luke walked right in. This wasn't abnormal. The boys acted like brothers and always walked in and out of each other's houses.

"I love Friday. What are you eating?" said Michael. As usual, Michael stuck his head in the fridge with Johnny and looked around as well. "How about string cheese?" he asked.

"That sounds good to me," said Johnny as he threw one to Luke and Michael.

The boys flopped down on the couch and pulled away at the cheese, dropping the strings into their mouths.

"Joey called and I'm supposed to call him back," Johnny said. "I wonder what he wants now?"

"He probably wants to switch topics and has a new way to ask Mrs. G," said Michael.

Johnny hopped off the couch, walked over to the kitchen and grabbed the phone. The kitchen was connected to the great room so the other boys turned to listen. Johnny dialed and waited for Joey to answer.

A muffled noise came over the phone. "Herro, Sbirelli rebidence."

Johnny started laughing and held his hand over the phone. "Hey guys, Joey's mouth is so full of food I can barely understand him." He removed his hand and added, "Joey is that you?"

"Yeah, it's me." Joey said. His voice was a beginning to get a little clearer. "I was eating a Ho-ho and a Ding-dong."

"At the same time?" Johnny asked.

"Yeah," Joey stated matter of factly. "Can you come over tomorrow? Ask Michael and Luke too. And can you guys bring your Lebron James books?"

"Sure," Johnny said. "I'll even bring over the rookie card and you can use it for your report. You'll have to guard it with your life, though."

"That would be great! I have something for you guys too," Joey said proudly. "I have some information that you can use."

"We'll be over at 9 a.m." Johnny hung up the phone.

"Joey wants to borrow our Lebron books and he has stuff for our report," Johnny told Luke and Michael.

A loud buzz came from the kitchen and Johnny's mom walked into the room.

"How about some monster cookies and milk?" she asked. With that the boys jumped up off the couch, hopped onto the loveseat, and bounded over the its back on their way to the kitchen.

"How about we take the cookies to the fort?" said Johnny.

With that suggestion the boys started humming the Bond theme song and shot each other with their finger pistols.

"Bond movies and monster cookies. What could be better?" said Luke.

CHAPTER SEVEN

Saturday was probably the nicest, warmest day that the boys had seen in a couple of months. The sun was already bright and moving upward in the sky. The boys peddled down Bridge Street on their BMX bikes, jumping over any obstacle that came in their way, or for that matter anything out of their way. Once one of the boys found a jump or a curb, the other two would follow and try to go higher or longer. Each would proclaim his jump the best and quickly move to the next obstacle.

Bridge Street was the oldest street in Mapleville, and though the three boys lived on the west side they were heading to east side that Joey lived on. The further east they rode, the older the houses were. Some of them dated back to the time when Mapleville was founded.

Joey Spinelli lived in one of those houses. It was a tall house with many peaks. The house was a light blue color with white trim. The tallest part of the house was a pointy dome topped with a weather vane that didn't spin any longer. On one side of the house was a huge fireplace made of brown stones. Joey's dad was always working on the house, which explained the ladders and scaffolding that always seemed to be outside. Next to the scaffolding was a truck with a large bucket attached to a crane.

The front door was the tallest that any of the boys had ever seen, and Joey Spaghetti was standing in it waiting for them. The huge door actually made Joey look small. True to form, his white shirt was covered with something red.

The boys jumped off their bikes and put their helmets on one of the handlebars. Johnny ran up the stairs first, as usual.

"What's up, Joey?" he said.

Joey looked up toward the sky and squinted his eyes. "I guess my dad is painting or something."

Johnny laughed to himself and Luke's shoulders shook a little like they usually did when he chuckled.

"He didn't really mean up – like up in the air," said Michael. "He meant how's it going?"

Joey dropped his head a little since he felt a kind of foolish. Actually, Joey was one of the smartest kids in the class. He loved to read and probably had read every book in the school library. At one point Mrs. Younkers, the school librarian, had to stop letting Joey check out books; she took away his library card because she complained that the books Joey borrowed were coming back full of crumbs or stained. Joey had to promise not to eat when he was reading library books and she agreed to let him have his card back.

"C'mon in guys," Joey said. "Let's go up to my room and hang out for a while."

The inside of the house was made of colorful woods and the ceilings were very high. Most of the furniture in the house was antique, or at least very old. The stairs were grand and made a large semi-circle up to the second floor.

"There has got to be fifty stairs to your room, Joey," said Johnny.

"Don't remind me," gasped Joey. "I have to walk these steps every day. But I do have the best view in the entire city."

Joey's house was on one of the biggest hills in town. From one of the windows you could see most of the downtown. The other window looked over Joey's back yard which was almost the length of a football field. His back yard sloped downward sharply to an area with a very large oak tree. Behind the tree was a graveyard that had been there for over one hundred years.

The graveyard was full of old tombs, most of them slanted or falling over. In the back of the graveyard was a very large tomb. It was the only one there and it kind of looked out of place. On the front of the tomb was the name Crebs. It was the tomb of Joey's great grandfather, Texas P. Crebs.

The boys knew that area well because a large flat field that they used for the baseball field lay beyond the graveyard. They spent endless summer hours playing on the field. Even Joey played baseball. He played catcher, of course, and had quite a good glove. That is, if the ball came close enough to him. If it didn't, it would roll to the backstop, which happened to be the back of Mr. Crebs' tomb.

Michael was looking out the window, daydreaming. "Basketball is over and soon it will be baseball season," he said.

"We are going to have to beat those knuckleheads again," said Luke. He was referring to the Hilltop Homers. That team was made up of the boys who played at Hilltop Park across town. Their leader was Rocky Jefferson, the meanest kid in all of Mapleville.

"It still makes me laugh when I think of how we won the summer slammer tournament," said Johnny.

The summer slammer tournament was held at the end of each summer, and last year the Bridge Street bombers beat the Homers 9 to 8 in the last inning when Michael hit a grand slam home run to end the game.

"How did you find out Rocky's real name anyway?" asked Luke.

Rocky, their best player, pitched for the Homers. Michael had yelled out Rocky's real name right when he pitched the ball to Michael. No one knew Rocky's real name until that exact moment. In fact, no one but Michael would have even dared to say it.

"My older brother went on a date with his older sister," said Michael. "She told him and he told me."

"I'll never forget the look on his face when you yelled out – Roscoe Fitzgerald Jefferson!" exclaimed Johnny. "I thought he was going to bean you."

"He was so surprised he threw you a meatball right down the middle of the plate!" said Luke. "I've never seen a ball hit that far!"

Michael, as usual, spread around the glory. "Well, if the three of you hadn't been on base then we wouldn't have won."

"Maybe this year we can get a real backstop instead of using your grandfather's tomb, Joey," said Johnny.

"He built that you know," said Joey. "I guess he could build just about anything including this house. My mom knows more about him than I do. She said he was a really smart man."

"I don't get it. Your last name is Spinelli and your great grandfather's name was Crebs," said Luke. "Am I missing something?"

"Yes silly, it's my mom's great grandfather. My dad married my mom after he opened his store and since the house belonged to my mom's family we get to live here," said Joey.

"Well, it is cool. And you have the best sliding banister I've ever seen," said Johnny.

"Let's go down to the kitchen. I'm hungry anyway," said Joey grabbing his stomach. "You guys can try out the banister that way."

CHAPTER EIGHT

Joey's kitchen always smelled wonderful. His mom was a great cook and since she'd married an Italian she was always cooking some sort of pasta. Even though it was early in the morning, she was stirring something in a big pot; it looked like spaghetti sauce.

"Hi, Mrs. Spinelli," the boys said almost in unison.

Just then Mrs. Spinelli raced over to the open window. "Anthony, be careful out there!" she yelled at Joey's dad.

"Oh my!" she said. "I don't know how your great grandfather took care of this house. It needs constant attention."

"He must have been a great builder," said Luke. "They don't build cool houses like this anymore."

"Yes, he was quite the man we are told. He was an inventor, a builder, and an engineer. He even knew a lot about history and wrote a lot of books on a number of subjects."

Just then Mr. Spinelli rushed past the kitchen window. He was in the bucket attached to the truck, operating it by a lever in the front of him.

Mrs. Spinelli went on. "What I know I learned from my grandmother and my mother. As far as we can tell he was some sort of genius."

Mr. Spinelli raced up and then down again, looking worried. He disappeared from view and the bucket dropped below the kitchen window. A can of paint followed him downward and flew out of sight as well.

Joey missed the whole thing, as his fingers were in the pot of sauce. The bucket slowly rose into view and Mr. Spinelli appeared, paint all over his head and dripping onto his face and clothes.

"Excuse me boys!" she exclaimed.

As she left the kitchen the boys heard her mumbling, "And to think he owns a hardware store. Hmmph!"

Joey looked up from the spaghetti pot and licked his fingers. "Let's go to the library and I'll get the stuff for your topic."

The boys walked out of the kitchen and down the hall to the library. It was the most amazing library the boys had ever seen in any house. Bookshelves stretched from floor to ceiling all around the room. There was a very old desk at one end of the room and a three foot globe stood in the center. Old leather couches were randomly placed around the library. At the other end of the room was an old telescope.

"There must be a thousand books in here," Johnny said. "No, ten thousand books! This room has to be twelve feet high."

"I think it's fourteen feet high, actually," said Joey.

The bookshelves were separated into ten levels each and a large ladder leaned against them. The ladder had rollers attached at the top and they rested on a bar that ran across the top of the bookshelves. It was used to access the books that were too high to reach.

"Here are the Lebron James books and rookie card," Michael said as he pulled them from the back-pack he was carrying.

"Thanks, and I've got some books for you guys too," said Joey. "Here they are."

Joey handed the boys an assortment of old books relating to gangs and horse thieves and bank robbers. They undoubtedly came from the Spinelli's library. The boys all plopped down on the couches and began to search through the books for the Baxter Bunch.

"Where did all these books come from?" asked Johnny.

"They have been here since my great grandfather owned the house," said Joey.

"It says here that the Baxter Bunch robbed a bank here in Mapleville and was never heard from again," said Michael.

"That's why I picked them for a topic. Imagine a bank robbery right here in Mapleville. How exciting!" exclaimed Joey.

"An NBA game here in Mapleville would be even more exciting!" Johnny shouted as he gave a high five to Luke.

"They were four brothers who robbed the First Mapleville Bank, and they stole eight thousand dollars in gold and currency," added Michael.

"Here it says that the money and gold were never recovered," said Luke.

"In my book, it talks about the brothers. The oldest was Specs Baxter, followed by Fuzzy, Quickdraw, and One-Eye," read Johnny. "It says that Specs was traveling by stagecoach from somewhere out East and when he arrived they hit the bank."

"I told you it would be a cool topic," said Joey.

"Listen to this, guys," said Michael. "Let me read the paragraph from the book: 'No one knows why Specs Baxter stooped to crime. He was a well renowned Professor from Stooksbury College in Massachusetts. His degrees included mathematics and engineering. Specs Baxter was instrumental in the building of the Larks Bay Bridge and some of the tallest buildings in Boston at the time.' "

"That's just weird," said Johnny. "Really weird."

Just then Mrs. Spinelli stuck her head in the door. "Joey, your father and I are going to head down to the store for more paint," she said. "I'll be back in time for lunch."

As she left the room, Joey leaned over the back of his couch and looked at the other boys.

"You want to see something weird?" he asked.

CHAPTER NINE

Joey walked over to the telescope and pointed it at the far end of the library. He bent over and stuck his eye onto the small lens and searched around for a moment. He pointed the telescope up almost as high as the ceiling, then waved the boys over to him.

"Look in here, guys," Joey said quietly.

Johnny, the first to look, peeked through the lens.

"It's pointed at some books, Joey. So what?" he said with a quizzical look on his face.

"Look closer this time," said Joey. "Look at the book."

Luke put his eye to the lens and stood there for a moment.

Then he replied, "It's a book called *Bank Robbers of the 1800s*. We have enough books. Why do we need another?"

"Do I have to tell you guys everything?" Joey said. "Who wrote the book for crying out loud?"

Michael took his turn and snapped up quickly, "Texas P. Crebs – hey that's your great grandfather!"

"Why are we looking at the book through a telescope anyway?" Johnny said. "Why didn't you give it to us like all the others?"

"I couldn't reach that one. The bar for the ladder is broken on that side of the library," Joey said. "I was playing with the telescope this morning and saw the book by accident just as you guys arrived."

With that, Johnny jumped over the couch toward the shelves and put his foot on the lowest one. He then scaled up a couple more, holding on to the wood between the shelves. Before long he was almost to the top and reaching to his left for the book.

"Careful, Johnny," said Luke. "I'm not playing shortstop if you get hurt."

Johnny inched his way toward the book and finally grasped it with his fingers. He pulled outward to remove the book and lost his grip. Johnny moved his feet higher and stood on a shelf so he was looking directly at the book. He grabbed the top of the book and gave it a tug.

"It's stuck," he said. "It won't budge."

"Yank on it," said Michael.

Johnny prepared himself to pull harder on the book. He grabbed the very top of the bookshelf with his left hand and the book with his right hand. He brought his feet up a little more to give himself some leverage. As he pulled back, there was a loud click and the book came flying backward. He barely held onto it with his right hand. At the same time his feet came off of the shelf and he was dangling by only his left hand.

"Look!" said Joey. "The whole bookshelf is open-ing like a door."

The bookshelf at the very end of the library slowly creaked open. Johnny was still dangling from the shelf

and went out of view as the bookshelf swung completely open.

"Wow, did you see that?" said Michael?

"I can't believe it!" said Luke. "It's a secret passageway!"

Michael, Luke, and Joey stood looking at the newly
opened bookshelf in amazement.

"Guys! Hey guys. I could use a little help up here,"
Johnny said as he hung from the shelf.

The boys quickly moved a couch underneath him
and he dropped onto it.

"I guess the book was some sort of trigger for the
secret passage," Johnny said.

Johnny handed the book to Joey and went over
to have a look. He peered to the right and saw some
stairs going downward.

"It's super dark in there. I can't see a thing," he
said. Joey turned around and ran out of the room. The
boys could hear his footsteps as he ran up the stairs
faster than they thought he could.

"Well, I don't blame him," said Luke. "It kind of
freaks me out too."

"He's the one who wanted to study the Baxter
Bunch," said Johnny.

The boys heard some noises upstairs followed by
footsteps coming down the grand stairs. Joey came
running into the room, breathing heavily. He was holding the book and four long objects.

"I got us some of these new flashlights that my dad
sells at the store," Joey gasped. "You crank the handle for a minute and you get light for almost an hour."

Joey handed out the flashlights and started cranking the handle. He pushed the button and a bright light gleamed through the lens.

"Let's go!" he exclaimed.

CHAPTER TEN

Joey pointed his flashlight down the stairs. The stairs and walls were made of brown stone. They seemed to go down forever. Joey moved into the opening and took the first step down the stairs.

"It kind of smells in here," he said. "It's dusty too."

Johnny entered next; he'd just finished cranking his light. He was followed by Luke and then Michael. The boys moved their lights up and down the stairs and around on the wall. With every step it got darker and darker in the narrow stairway.

"Without these lights, I wouldn't be able to see my nose!" said Luke. "Maybe we should go get some help or something."

"Awww, c'mon Luke, nothing is going to happen. It's just a bunch of stairs," said Joey as he continued down the steps.

The boys walked down until they were definitely below the level of the basement.

Joey stopped. "The steps end here. There is a small passageway up ahead," he said.

Stuck into the wall above them was a metal rod with the end bent almost into a circle. Joey aimed his light ahead and saw another one.

"I wonder what those are for?" he asked.

"Maybe they're for a torch," Johnny said. "That way they could light up the passageway."

"I bet you're right," said Michael.

The passageway was dusty with lots of cobwebs. Some rocks that must have come loose from the walls or ceiling littered the floor.

The boys moved down the passage until they reached a small room with smooth walls. It had a doorway on the other side. The boys stopped in the middle of the room.

"What is this place?" asked Michael.

"No idea," said Johnny, "but it must lead some-where because there is another door."

The boys were standing in a small circle with their flashlights shining at each other's faces. The rest of the room was completely dark.

"I say we go back," said Luke.

"What could happen? It's just another hallway," pleaded Joey. He turned around and started down the new passageway. Just as he took his first step, they heard a noise from underneath his foot. The click triggered something behind them in the passageway they had just left. Just as the boys turned around, a large door-like rock fell from the ceiling.

"The passageway is blocked!" yelled Michael.

"What could happen? What could happen? I'll tell you what could happen. We could get trapped down here!" Luke screamed.

"It's okay, Luke. We'll get out of here. Besides, Joey's Mom and Dad said they will be back by lunch. They will find us," Johnny said, trying to calm him down.

"Don't worry. We'll be fine," Joey said. "There is only one way to go now. I think we should move ahead."

The boys nodded in agreement and slowly walked down the next passage. It was about as long as the first and ended in a room just like other. Joey turned around before he entered the room. The other boys bumped into each other with the abrupt stop.

"This time when I leave the room I'll be more careful and not step on any trigger stones," Joey said. "What can happen?"

"Quit saying that," said Luke from behind Johnny.

Joey stepped backward into the middle of the room. He didn't see it coming. The middle part of the floor disappeared and Joey dropped out of sight down a trap door. The boys gasped as they heard Joey screaming for what seemed like a minute. The last of Joey's voice echoed as if he had fallen down a well.

"Joey! Joey, can you hear us?" The boys were screaming.

Nothing. No light. No sound. Nothing.

Joey had fallen down what looked like a metal chute of some kind. The three boys stood there for a moment looking down the hole onto the chute when suddenly the trap door sprang shut.

"Aw man, we gotta find Joey," said Michael. "I'm not going down that chute to find him, though."

Johnny was on his knees shining his flashlight at the edges where the trapdoor had opened. "The dust was disturbed where the door was, so I think we can go around it safely. I say we keep going and maybe the path will lead us to him."

"Alright, but let's go really slowly," said Luke. The boys inched their way around the outside of the room far away from the trapdoor's edges. When they reached the other side, they moved slowly into another passageway.

CHAPTER ELEVEN

"Baby steps, baby steps," pleaded Luke. "I don't want to see any more rocks fall from the ceiling."

The boys inched further and further into the depths of the secret passageway. After painstakingly feeling every inch of the floor with their hands, they finally reached an opening. The three boys stepped into the doorway and lit the area in front of themselves with the flashlights. There was a large ledge where they were standing and by their feet were rocks and small boulders. A rope and some wooden crates lay on their left. Directly in front of them was what seemed to be a small bridge standing upright, pointing into the air. Beyond the bridge lay a chasm of darkness that the boys' flashlights couldn't seem to penetrate.

"That's a deep hole!" said Johnny. "But I can see a ledge on the other side."

"The bridge seems long enough to make it to the other side," said Michael. "Maybe if we push it over we can cross the gap."

The three boys situated themselves behind the bridge and pushed lightly at first, not knowing what would happen. They increased their efforts, only to realize that the bridge wasn't going to move.

"Darn it! It's stuck!" said Luke. "It's just got to move. Why would someone build a bridge that stands straight up in the air?"

"Maybe there is a latch or lever or something to release it," Michael said hopefully.

The flashlights were moving in all directions, searching for something to release the bridge.

"Here!" Luke exclaimed. "There's a different colored rock on the wall."

Behind them on the wall they saw what seemed to be a button. It was about three feet off the ground, slightly rounded, and stuck out from the rest of the wall.

"Push it!" said Johnny.

Luke pushed harder and harder until the rock moved. Mechanical sounds of gears startled the boys, and soon the bridge started downward until it met the other ledge across from where they were standing.

"Alright, let's go," said Michael as he started across the bridge. The metal bridge was sturdy and the boys walked across. Just as Luke took his last step off the bridge, it started to elevate and soon returned to its former position.

"Well, I guess it doesn't matter anyway. Let's just keep moving," Johnny said.

Luke knelt and looked closely at the ledge. He put his flashlight on the ground and dug around with his fingers.

"There was a latch here to hold the bridge down, but it was filled with dirt," he stated as he dug the rest of the dirt away. "You're right though, Johnny. Let's go."

The boys moved into the doorway and found another large stairway with steps that reached further into the earth. Johnny cranked his flashlight, as the power was starting to decrease. They moved slowly down and reached another opening. Johnny was the first one through the doorway into the next room.

"Oh no!" Johnny exclaimed. "There was a bridge here but it's gone!"

A rocky bridge that had once spanned the gap had collapsed and broken away. A few feet of the rocky bridge was left on each side, but the middle section had disappeared into the depths below.

"Now what?" said Michael. "There is no way we can jump that far. It's got to be ten feet!"

On their side of the room were rocks and a few wooden crates but nothing to span the gap. Johnny sat down on one of the crates to think. Luke paced back and forth.

"We need something to get us across," said Luke. "Like a long board or something."

"What we need is James Bond. He would have some sort of gadget that would fire a rope across and climb to the other side," Johnny said.

Michael pointed his light at Johnny and shouted, "That's it. A rope! There was a rope back beyond the last bridge!"

"We can't get the rope, Michael. The bridge went back up, remember?" said Luke.

"Well we have to try, don't we?" Michael pleaded.

The boys knew that it was their only hope. They marched back up the long stairs into the opening.

"Grab some rocks and maybe we can hit the trigger," Johnny said. "We are going to have to hit it really hard."

The boys tried to hit the rock that stuck out of the wall. They hit the trigger rock a few times, but not with enough force to get it to move. Johnny sat down on another one of the crates when his arm began to tire.

"It's no use. I can't hit it hard enough to go in," said Johnny. "We will never find Joey this way."

Michael, the pitcher for the Bridge Street Bombers, was still throwing as hard as he could. Eventually, he sat down next to Johnny and the crate collapsed. Johnny pulled a piece of the board out from under him and turned his head a little.

"Rocket shot! Rocket shot!" Johnny shouted.

"Yeah, Rocket shot!" Michael repeated. "That will do it!"

Johnny handed the piece of wood to Luke, and Michael handed him a small rock. The two of them aimed their flashlights to give Luke the most light to see. Luke raised the board high over his head and tossed up the rock. With a mighty swing, he connected and shot the small round rock toward the trigger. It connected with a loud "crack" and the boys heard the mechanical gears engage. The bridge lowered slowly until it clicked into the latch that Luke had cleaned out earlier.

"Rocket shot!" they all yelled. They put their fists together without saying anything else.

Johnny ran and retrieved the rope and they all started back down the stairs.

CHAPTER TWELVE

The rope was about thirty feet long and although it was old it seemed to be sturdy. Johnny grabbed the one end of the rope and coiled it neatly on the ground.

"What now?" said Luke. "How are we going to get the rope across?"

Michael aimed his light across to the other ledge, looking for something to connect the rope. He moved his light forward and then backward and then forward again. He then grabbed one of the crates and carried it to the wall behind them.

"I can tie one end of the rope to the torch holder on this side," he said, "but how are we going to attach it to the other side?"

Johnny grabbed the end of the rope and tied a loop in it. He started swinging it over his head and let it fly toward the other side. The looped end of the rope missed badly and dropped down into the darkness.

"That's not going to work," he said. "It's not heavy enough."

Johnny tried a couple more times with the same effect. Luke and Michael each tried once, but nobody even came close to the torch holder.

Luke picked up a rock and held it up in one hand. "Hey, what about tying a rock to the end?"

"Yeah, you could throw the rock and if you did it just right the rope could slip in between the metal, and the rock would get wedged underneath the torch holder," said Johnny.

He took the rock from Luke and began to tie the rock to the rope. It took several tries before they got the rock tied tightly to the rope without it falling out. Johnny lifted the rock and rope and handed them to Michael.

"It's kind of heavy," Johnny said with a bit of concern.

Michael started to swing the rock a little, trying to figure out how he was going to get it across to the other side.

Johnny leaned over and spoke softly. "Hey, Michael, shoot a three-pointer."

Michael stopped swinging the rope and took the rock in both hands. He brought the rock way down to his right and with all his might shot the rock into the air. The rock made an arc over the gap and the rope uncoiled as it flew. The rock glanced off the wall directly behind the torch holder and the rope barely slid into the opening in the semi-circle. When it came to rest, the rock was dangling a couple of feet below the torch holder.

"Three-pointer! Three-pointer!" The boys danced around as they screamed.

Johnny looked down just as the last of the rope was sliding off the edge of the ledge. He dove toward the rope and his arms disappeared over the edge. Michael and Luke looked over with dismay. Johnny stood up slowly with the rope in his hands.

"Whew, that was close," he gasped. "Now we will have to see if the rock will hold."

He slowly drew back on the rope until the rock was just underneath the torch holder. He gave it one last tug and since the rock was slightly larger than the circular ring it wedged itself tightly.

"Here, now tie it off on the torch holder on this side," Johnny said as he handed the rope to Michael.

Michael climbed up on the crate and tied it off as tightly as he could. Johnny put his flashlight in his back pocket and walked out onto the few feet of remaining bridge. He reached up for the rope and slowly lifted his feet off the ground. Hand over hand, he steadily moved across. When he was well over the other ledge, he dropped down safely.

"No sweat, guys," Johnny said confidently. "It's just like the monkey bars at school."

Luke and Michael crossed the gap as easily as Johnny and afterwards they quietly celebrated by touching knuckles.

"Press on," said Michael as he walked into the next opening.

The next passageway was quite short and it opened into a small circular area followed by long narrow room. Michael walked into the circular room first, followed by Johnny. As soon as Luke stepped in, the floor shifted downward about an inch.

"Not again," said Luke. "Not another trigger rock! I can't take much more of this."

The boys turned toward the narrow room after they heard the humming sound of wheels and gears. They aimed their flashlights in the direction of a series of metal pendulums connected to large stones. There were six in all, three moving from the right and three from the left. The stones swung back and forth, alternating from each direction. It was a passageway that was seemingly impossible to cross.

"I see another one of those trigger stones on the far wall," Luke said, pointing his flashlight in that direction.

"How about hitting another rock at it?" Michael questioned.

"Never work. Too many of those swinging things in the way," Luke responded.

Johnny was staring at the swinging rocks. His eyes looked almost glazed with determination. Just then, he pulled back his right foot and pushed off in order to get a good start.

"Johnny! No!" Luke screamed. "You'll get crushed!"

Johnny went left and right and then left and then right again. Each time his body went to a side he swung his hips to avoid being hit by the swinging rock. He looked a lot like when he moved the basketball up the court. He went left and right once more and dove past the last pendulum. Johnny stood up, brushed himself off and pushed the trigger rock which promptly stopped the swinging.

Luke and Michael moved to the other side of the passageway to join Johnny, as it was now easy to pass.

"The Weave, right?" Michael said to Johnny.

"Nice one!" said Luke.

The boys touched knuckles once again.

CHAPTER THIRTEEN

The next opening wound down a bunch of stairs that seemed to go forever. Luke broke the silence when he yelled, "I see a light up ahead."

The boys picked up the pace and made their way toward the light.

"Shhh," Johnny whispered. "The light is moving around. Turn off your flashlights."

They inched their way toward a large hole in the ground. The light was moving around in different directions and a whirring sound came from the hole. When they came to the edge they all turned on their lights at once. Near the bottom of the hole cranking his flashlight was Joey Spaghetti!

A rope netting hung maybe a foot or two beneath him. Joey seemed to be fine but was somewhat tangled up.

"Can't you climb out?" asked Johnny. "You are only three feet down."

"Umm, not really," said Joey. "Besides, I knew you guys would be here soon. It was the coolest slide I've ever been on in my life!"

Michael and Luke jumped into the net to help Joey get to his feet and climb out. As Joey stood up, he motioned to Johnny above him.

"Here, catch this," Joey said, tossing his great grandfather's book.

"You still have this thing?" Johnny said as he opened his hands.

The book flew upward and when Johnny grabbed it he heard a rattling noise not usually associated with a book. Luke and Michael got underneath Joey and heaved him over the edge.

"I think there is something in this book," stated Johnny.

He pulled open the front cover to reveal a secret compartment.

"What's in there?" said Joey.

'Hmm, an antique pair of glasses and a really old picture," Johnny said.

The boys gathered around and aimed their flash-lights toward the image. Four men who looked like cowboys stood next to each other in front of an old building. The one on left with glasses and a beard was definitely the oldest, and the three to the right looked younger and rougher.

"There is some writing under each of them. It must be their names," Luke said as he looked a little closer. "The guy on the left is Specs Baxter, followed by Fuzzy, Quickdraw, and One-Eye!"

"How cool!" Joey exclaimed as he grabbed the picture to see for himself.

When he held it up, Johnny noticed some writing on the back of the picture.

"Read the back, Joey," he said.

Joey turned the picture over and read the writing on the back.

"It says: 'If one could look through my eyes, one could know the truth'," read Joey.

"This gets weirder by the minute," said Luke.

"By the way, any of you guys have anything to eat?" asked Joey. "It's got to be getting close to lunchtime. I'm starving."

The boys shook their heads and headed down the next corridor.

CHAPTER FOURTEEN

"There is some light up ahead!" said Luke. "A lot of light!"

The four boys moved along quickly and entered a large, shiny, stone-walled room that had light coming in from above. In the center of the room stood a pedestal embedded with a large crystal prism. Across from where the boys entered rose a large metal spiral stairway. What looked like coffins on short stone bases sat in three corners of the room. The fourth corner had the same stone base, but an old safe was placed on top of it.

"What is this place?" said Michael. He was not expecting an answer.

Johnny walked over to one of the stone coffins. He peered over the top and read from the inscription plate on the wall.

"This one says One-Eyed Baxter. Died 1881," read Johnny.

Luke read from the other corner. "Fuzzy Baxter over here. He died in 1881 too."

Michael walked to the last coffin and read the writing. "Quickdraw Baxter. Died 1881."

"How come there are only three?" questioned Joey. "Where's Specs Baxter?"

Johnny moved in the direction of the last stone base with the safe on it. He looked at the safe and then noticed that there was a plate above it.

"Well, he's supposed to be right here. The plate says Specs Baxter. The only difference is it doesn't say when he died," said Johnny, "and he has a safe where his coffin should be."

Luke walked over to Johnny and leaned forward to look at the safe more closely.

"Hey guys, this safe is from the First Mapleville Bank. I bet the Baxter Bunch took it when they robbed the place!"

Luke tried to turn the lever on the front of the safe, but it wouldn't budge.

"This is very cool but I'm starving, guys!" pleaded Joey. "Let's get out of here and get something to eat! It's got to be noon by now. After we have lunch we can get some tools from my dad's hardware store and open the safe."

The boys agreed and made their way to the metal staircase. None of them had noticed that there was a gated door with an empty keyhole in the front.

"It's locked and we're trapped," said Joey. "Now I'm really starving."

"We know you're starving, Joey," answered Johnny.

The boys slid down one by one with their backs to the gate and leaned back.

"I just can't figure it out. There has got to be a way out of here," said Luke.

Ten minutes passed without a word, and the only noise that could be heard was the grumbling of Joey's stomach. More light began to enter the room from above; it was almost as bright as it would be outside.

All of a sudden the light seemed to concentrate on the prism on the pedestal in the middle of the room. The boys stood up, knowing that something was different. The crystal seemed to be about ready to explode when beams of light shot out in five streams throughout the room. Four of the light beams were focused on the inscription plates and the last one was focused on another part of the wall, an area the boys hadn't examined. Michael was waving his hand in and out of the light beam. "Look at the light!" he said with amazement.

Joey wasn't as impressed. He cried out, "The lights aren't going to get us out of here. I'm hungry."

Johnny walked over by Joey and took the picture from him. He turned it over and read it again.

He started mumbling to himself, " 'If one could look through my eyes' . . . Joey, give me those glasses!"

Johnny put on the glasses and spun around, looking at each beam of light and where it was aimed. He stopped when he came to the beam pointed at Specs Baxter's plate.

"That's odd! When you look at Specs' name plate through these glasses it says Texas P. Crebs," Johnny said.

"That's your great grandfather Joey!" exclaimed Luke.

"The other beams don't change anything except the one pointed at the wall and it shows three numbers . . . 21-16-46."

"The combination to the safe!" yelled Joey.

Michael ran over to the safe and began to spin the dial to unlock the safe. He turned the lever and heard a click. He pulled open the door and reached inside.

CHAPTER FIFTEEN

"There's a key and it's attached to a note," Michael said.

"Read it," said Joey. "Read it."

" 'To whom it may concern,' " Michael started. " 'I was wrongly accused of helping my brothers rob the First Mapleville Bank. The truth is that I was still on a stagecoach on the way to Mapleville when the bank was robbed.' "

Michael went on, " 'My brothers took the safe and were about to break into it near an old graveyard when the ground apparently gave way underneath them and they fell into a cave to their deaths. I found them and knew that no one would believe that I hadn't played a part in the crime. I decided to build the tomb over them to hide the truth. I shaved my beard and changed my appearance to hide from the law. Please take notice that none of the gold or money is missing. I am sorry for my criminal brothers' actions.' "

"That's amazing," said Johnny.

"Wait, it was signed Specs Baxter AND Texas P. Crebs!" added Michael.

"Oh my gosh!" exclaimed Joey. "My great grand-father was Specs Baxter! I should have figured it out!"

"What do you mean?" asked Johnny.

"It's an anagram. Don't you see?" said Joey.

"What's an anagram?" asked Michael.

"Don't you remember Mrs. G taught us about anagrams in class? It's when you scramble the exact same letters of one word to make another," Johnny explained.

"Or in my great grandfather's case, he took the letters of his name and scrambled them to form another one," Joey Spaghetti stated. "You see – Specs Baxter scrambled up is Texas P. Crebs. It's an anagram."

Luke pointed at the safe. He grabbed a gold coin and held it up for the other boys to see. "I wonder how much this is worth now."

Michael untied the string holding the key to the note and walked over to the locked gate.

"I bet this leads right up to your great grandfather's tomb," he said confidently.

The light began to dim in the room and the beams of lights turned off almost like a light switch.

"I think it's time to go," said Johnny. "I've had enough excitement for one day."

Michael unlocked the gate and the boys started the climb up the spiral metal stairs.

CHAPTER SIXTEEN

Johnny was leaning back on the bed next to Michael, and Luke was on the top bunk. Just as James Bond was going to kiss a girl, the boys heard someone calling them from outside.

"Hey guys!" yelled Joey Spaghetti.

Johnny, Luke, and Michael all tried to stick their heads out of the sliding window at once.

"Hey, Joey. What are you doing here?" asked Johnny.

"My mom and dad drove me over and we are all gonna have a picnic," said Joey. "Mom made some pasta!"

The boys started to laugh to each other, since Joey's mom always had pasta or spaghetti.

"Oh by the way – my dad returned the money and gold to the First Mapleville Bank," said Joey. "And there's a reward!"

"A reward?" asked Luke.

"Yep and my dad says it will be enough to build a baseball field with dugouts and a real backstop!" Joey said as he started to walk away. "I'll meet you guys up at the house."

Johnny, Luke and Michael pulled their heads back into the fort just as the movie was ending. The theme song started up. Like always, they started humming and shooting each other. When they were finished, Johnny stuck out his arm and made a fist. Luke made one, followed by Michael.

"A new ball field," Johnny said.

"With dugouts," said Luke.

"And a real backstop," added Michael.

"KNUCKLES!" they screamed. "KNUCKLES!"

Stormy Weathers

To all the boys on the fishing trip - young and old

CHAPTER ONE

It was an unusually hot day, and the sun was shining heavily on the outside of the fort. Johnny, Luke, and Michael were relaxing after a morning spent playing catch.

Michael had been practicing his pitching for the upcoming Summer Slammer baseball tournament, with Luke and Johnny taking turns catching for him. By noon the three of them were tired and hungry.

"Boys, lower the bucket," called Johnny's mom. "I have sandwiches and sodas for you."

Johnny stuck his head out of the sliding window of the fort as the other two boys worked the pulley that lowered the bucket.

"Thanks, Mom!" replied Johnny. "You're the best!"

The boys unloaded the lunch and spread it out over the lower bunk.

"I'm starved," said Michael as he took the first bite of his sandwich.

"Hey, Johnny, we should turn on a movie," said Luke.

Johnny jumped up off the bed and put a movie into the DVD player.

"I think we will watch the first James Bond film," he stated. "My dad likes this one the best."

The boys sat back on the bed and began another of the series of James Bond movies, as they always did in the fort. They all waited quietly in anticipation of the theme song, which would send them into a frenzy of pretending to shoot each other while humming along with the music. Today was slightly more subdued as none of them wanted to knock over the food and soda on the bed.

After finishing up their lunch, the three boys lay back on the bed. One by one they dozed off due to the effects of the baseball, the heat, and their full stomachs.

Suddenly, they were startled by a knocking noise at the bottom of the fort. Johnny jumped off the bed and tried to peek through a crack near the door.

"Password," he demanded.

"What? Johnny, you know I don't know the password!" Johnny's dad said.

Johnny's dad and grandfather had built the fort the summer before, placing it on four large posts close to the large oak tree in the corner of the yard. The outside of the fort was pretty simple, but the boys didn't care. It was the cool stuff on the inside that they liked. The bunk bed and DVD, along with the television set that Mr. Beardsley had given them, made it a great place to hang out.

"Oh, hi Dad!" said Johnny. "The password this week is 'grand slam' in case you wanted to know."

The boys had the habit of changing the passwords often in order to keep out trespassers, especially girls.

"Hey Dad, you're home early aren't you?" Johnny asked.

"Sure am! I have to get all the gear ready for the fishing trip," Johnny's dad said.

The boys were all sticking their heads out of the small opening in the sliding window. It was quite a sight as the space was big enough for maybe two of them.

"I just wanted to know if you wanted to help. You can help me pack the trailer," said Johnny's dad.

"I had better get home too. My dad said he was coming home early to get ready," stated Michael. "He's been packing for a whole week!"

"My dad's been doing the same!" added Luke. "You would think we were going away for a month!"

"I'll help for sure Dad!" said Johnny. "But I can only help for awhile. We play the Clark Street Cubbies tonight in the first round of the Summer Slammer tournament. If we win, we won't play again until we get back from our trip."

The Summer Slammer tournament was held at the end of every summer. All of the neighborhood teams from all over Mapleville would enter. Johnny, Michael, and Luke played for the Bridge Street Bombers. The Bombers were the favorites to win the tournament, but they would still have to get by Rocky Jefferson and the Hilltop Homers. Luckily, the Bombers wouldn't have to meet them unless they both reached the finals.

The boys jumped down from the ladder and went to help their dads pack for the trip. For the next hour or so, Johnny handed his dad sleeping bags, fishing poles, tackle, and duffle bags full of clothing.

"Gotta go Dad!" Johnny said. "The game is gonna start soon."

"Good luck to the Bombers!" his dad shouted.

CHAPTER TWO

Even though Clark Street was all the way across town, the boys rode their bikes to the park as usual. Just as they arrived, Joey Spinelli, Danny J and Danny R were getting out of Mrs. Spinelli's car. The rest of the team was already warming up.

"Are these guys any good?" asked Danny J.

"They're not bad, but their pitcher is awesome!" said Luke. "He throws a pretty mean fastball."

"His name is Mark Temple," said Michael. "He beaned me by accident once and I had a goose egg on my head for a week."

"It should be a low scoring game. They aren't going to be able to hit Michael, so they won't score much," stated Johnny. "One or two runs could win the game."

The game progressed just about like Johnny predicted. The score was two to two and it was the bottom of the last inning. Michael had hit two home runs, but that was all the scoring the Bombers could manage. Mark Temple was still throwing very fast and showed no signs of slowing down.

"I hurt my wrist a little diving for that last ball," said Michael.

"Well, if we score a run you won't need to hit anyway. You're up fourth this inning," said Johnny.

Joey Spinelli struck out on three fastballs for the first out. Johnny was up next and figured he would get a fastball too. He connected nicely and smacked the ball to left field for a single.

"Hit him in, Luke. I'm not sure if I can bat because of my wrist," Michael said quietly before Luke headed to the plate. "He might throw you a curve since Johnny hit his fastball."

Luke walked up to the plate, tapped his shoes with his bat, and got ready for what he hoped would be a curve. Mark leaned back to make his delivery and flipped his wrist to throw a curve. Luke saw it coming and swung as hard as he could. The bat made a loud "crack!" and the ball sailed out toward center field. Johnny was moving down toward second, waiting to see how far the ball would go. Tiny Pearson, the Cubbies centerfielder, was running as fast as he could toward the fence. Tiny was the smallest kid on his team, but he was surprisingly fast.

The entire Bombers team was screaming "Home run!" when little Tiny Pearson stuck his foot into the fence and jumped into the air. He stuck his glove up over the fence and made the best catch that any of the boys had ever seen. It became very quiet on the Bombers' bench.

Michael slowly walked up to the plate, rubbing his wrist a little. Johnny took a big lead at first and Mark Temple wound up for his pitch. Johnny broke toward second base without looking back. The pitch was in the dirt and the catcher had no chance of throwing Johnny out at second.

Mark Temple wasn't too worried about Johnny, since he only had to get Michael out to send the game into extra innings. The Cubbies weren't paying attention to Johnny, who took advantage of the chance to dart for third on the next delivery. Michael swung at the pitch and missed, but Johnny, who was the fastest boy on the team, was safe again.

Just then, Luke unexpectedly walked out and called timeout. Michael and Johnny walked over and met him between third base and home.

"What's going on, Luke?" asked Michael.

"I got an idea that just might work," said Luke eagerly. "I think you should bunt, Michael."

"Bunt?" questioned Johnny. "Are you serious?"

"Yeah, I'm serious! I saw it on television the other night. It's called a squeeze play," explained Luke. "Johnny steals home when the pitch is thrown and Michael bunts the ball right past him. Just make sure you are safe at first, Michael."

"I think it's worth a try," said Michael. "I don't think I could hit the ball too hard with my hand this way."

The boys all made fists and touched them together. It was the unofficial handshake of the fort and they used it now to wish each other good luck.

"Knuckles," they said somewhat quietly.

Michael returned to the plate and pointed his bat to the outfield. Everyone on both teams was waiting in anticipation of the duel between pitcher and batter.

As Mark Temple reared back, Johnny took off toward home plate. Michael lifted his bat as if he were getting ready to make a swing and then lowered his bat quickly into a bunting stance. The Cubbies' third basemen was caught off guard and wasn't ready to charge the ball.

Michael bunted the ball perfectly down the third base line and it passed Johnny to his left. Johnny sprung forward and dove for home. The third basemen grabbed the ball and threw it home after Johnny had already touched the plate to score.

The catcher, who was also surprised, took a little too much time before he realized he had to try to throw Michael out at first. Everyone in the park could clearly hear Michael's foot hit the bag before the ball slapped into the first basemen's glove.

"We win! We win!" the Bombers yelled, piling on top of each other.

The boys shook hands with the other team and congratulated each other on a fine game.

"That squish play worked really great, Luke," said Michael.

Johnny and Luke looked at each other and chuckled.

"Squeeze play!" exclaimed Luke.

The three boys laughed all the way home as they rode their bikes through Mapleville.

CHAPTER THREE

"Five o'clock in the morning is too early to get up," stated Luke.

Michael and Johnny nodded.

The boys jumped in the car carrying their backpacks. It was still dark outside, and even a little chilly for summer. They were all wearing shorts but covered up with their sleeping bags in the back of the car.

"How long do we have to drive?" said Johnny.

"It's about twelve hours or so," said Johnny's dad. "That's why we have to leave so early."

Michael looked like he had just rolled out of bed, as his curly hair was a complete mess. "I think I'll sleep all the way," he said. "Wake me when we get to Canada!"

The boys and their dads all laughed as the car pulling the trailer made its way out of the driveway.

"What's the name of the fishing camp, Dad?" asked Johnny.

"The place is named Stormy's Fish Camp," said Johnny's dad. "We will be fishing for walleyes and northern pike."

"I can taste those fish sandwiches already!" exclaimed Luke's dad. "There is nothing like fresh walleye!"

The three boys looked at each other with disgust.

Luke finally yelled, "Gross! I hope you guys brought hot dogs. I don't think I will be able to eat any fish."

"Are you kidding?" said Michael's dad. "Fish is brain food, but you knuckleheads wouldn't know that because you don't eat fish!"

The three boys pulled out their hand-held electronic devices and played as long as they could before their eyes got heavier. They all slept on and off for most of the ride until they finally pulled into the parking lot of Stormy's Fishing Lodges.

"We're here!" yelled Luke. "Let's go fishing!"

"Where is our cabin?" asked Johnny as he scrambled to get out of the car.

"Wait a minute. Slow down," said his dad. "We don't get to go to the lodge until tomorrow morning. This is just the starting point in order to fly to the lodge."

"We get to fly?" screamed Michael. "That's awesome!"

"Yep, see those float planes in the water over there? We will be taking one of those tomorrow morning," said Johnny's dad. "Now let's unload what we need because we are staying in the hotel next door for the night."

CHAPTER FOUR

Stormy's Fishing Lodges' office opened at five a.m. and was busy every morning of the fishing season. People came from all over to board a float plane to take them to their remote fishing destination. The building was mostly a souvenir store, with a long desk in the back. Around the inside of the store were numerous stuffed animals and fish and even a set of what looked like cowboy pistols attached to a plaque on the wall. A younger women and an older man stood behind the counter. A little girl wandering around the office with some papers in her hand smiled at the boys as she walked outside. The man wore a shirt that said Stormy's Fishing Lodges, and the boys walked up to him.

"Are you Stormy?" said Johnny.

"Can we go now?" questioned Michael.

"Is it a long plane ride?" asked Luke.

The man looked down at the boys and pointed his index finger as if he were shooting at them. "No, no, and no," he said in a somewhat unfriendly tone.

"Is that a stuffed grizzly bear?" Johnny wondered.

"Is that a walleye?" Michael said as he pointed to the wall.

"What kind of guns are those?" asked Luke.

The older man stopped and peered over the counter at the boys. He spoke slowly and a little more loudly than before. "No, no, and a forty-four, a Colt .44. It's a type of pistol. I've got lots of people waiting to go to their fishing destinations. Now unless you boys leave me alone to get my work done, I might have to get one of my pistols off the wall, if you know what I mean."

The younger woman quickly moved from behind the counter and put her arms around the boys while she moved them to the other side of the store.

"Don't pay any attention to him. He can be a little ornery in the morning," she said. "What are your names?"

"My name's Michael, and this is Johnny and Luke," Michael said as he pointed to the other boys.

"Well, my name is Mary, Mary Weathers and I'm happy to meet you," Mary said. "How about, since we got off to a rough start around here, I'll give you each of you boys a free sweatshirt."

"Awesome!" said Luke.

Mary helped each of the boys find their size and answered their questions about the stuffed fish and animals around the store.

"Who is that old man anyway?" asked Johnny. "He doesn't seem very nice."

Mary gathered the boys together and whispered, "His name is Frank Hilmer and you are right, Johnny. He isn't very nice. He's just plain grumpy."

"Then why do you work here?" asked Luke.

"Well, that is a very good question," she said. "I suppose it's because this is the only job I know. I guess the real reason is that my father helped to start this place."

Mary looked up into the air and didn't say anything more.

"Hey Mary, you're not giving away any more sweatshirts, are you?" Frank yelled angrily from across the store.

"No, don't worry about us over here, Frank," Mary answered back.

She whispered again to the boys, "It will be our little secret. Don't say anything about the sweatshirts."

Just then the little girl who had smiled at the boys earlier walked up. "Hi," she said.

"Johnny, Luke, and Michael, this is my daughter, Meredith," said Mary. "Why don't you take the boys to the restaurant to get some breakfast and I'll come get you all when they are ready to go."

"Ok, Mom," she replied. "Hey guys, follow me."

Meredith and the boys started to walk out the front door when they heard Frank yell from the counter. "Did those boys pay for those sweatshirts?"

"All taken care of, Frank," Meredith answered without looking back. She hurried a little and flew out the door.

CHAPTER FIVE

The restaurant was extremely busy for so early in the morning. Most of the tables were full of people waiting to fly out for their fishing trips. Some of the tables had locals just eating their breakfast before heading off to work. Meredith and the boys found a table with a view of the lake where the float planes were being loaded with fishing gear. Soon the waitress walked up to the table with a pen and paper.

"Hi Meredith, who are your friends?" she asked.

"This is Johnny, Luke, and Michael. They are going on a fishing trip for a few days," Meredith said. "They are going to have some breakfast before they go."

"Well, it's my pleasure to meet you," said the waitress. "I think you guys would like our classic. It's eggs, bacon, toast, and orange juice."

After everyone agreed she said, "I'll be back in a minute . . . and by the way, you boys are gonna have a blast at the lake!" The waitress smiled at the boys and walked off to the kitchen.

Just then, Meredith stood up and waved at a burly man who had just walked into the restaurant. He wore a bright red suit with lots of gold buttons and a very wide brimmed hat. He walked over to the table and removed his hat.

"Hey guys, this is Bill Donaldson. He is one of the Royal Canadian Mounted Police," Meredith said.

"It's very nice to meet you. I hope you enjoy your stay in Canada," said Bill. "If you need any help from the Mounties while you are here, just let me know. I'm usually here for breakfast every day!"

The boys stood up and shook Bill's hand before he walked to a table across the restaurant where another Mountie was sitting.

"Wow, everyone is so nice here," said Johnny, "except for that Frank guy."

"Yep, you are right, Johnny," Meredith said. "My mom doesn't like working for him but she practically runs the place so it would be hard for her to leave. Plus, my grandpa used to own part of the place, until he didn't come back one time."

"What do you mean?" asked Luke.

"Well it's kind of a long story, but since you guys aren't going anywhere," Meredith said, "I'll tell you."

Meredith leaned forward a little and started to tell the boys about her grandfather.

"Everyone called him Stormy. No one really knows why, but it sounded kind of funny when they used his last name. Weathers – Stormy Weathers. Get it?" she asked.

"It's kind of corny, but go on," said Michael.

"Well, my grandpa, Stormy had a cabin on Pelican Lake, where you guys are going actually. He owned all the land around that area," Meredith said. "He and

Frank decided to become partners in a fishing lodge operation. They built some extra cabins and some docks, and things were going pretty well."

The waitress walked up and served the breakfasts to the kids. Meredith waited to begin again until she left.

"Where was I? Oh yeah. Frank and Stormy were up fishing at Stormy's cabin," Meredith went on. "Stormy went out and got caught in some bad weather and never came back."

"Did he drown?" asked Johnny.

"No one knows," said Meredith. "It's so mysterious. I never met my grandpa, but everyone says he was a real outdoorsman. The Royal Canadian Mounties looked for days, but they never found any sign of him. I guess it was very odd."

The boys were so interested that they had barely eaten any of their food.

"The weirdest thing is that Frank came back alone, and then it turned out that he and Stormy had signed an agreement that if one of them died the other would get the business," Meredith said. "My mom would actually own half of the company if my grandpa wouldn't have done that."

"That's a bummer," said Luke.

"I know. I think she keeps hoping that she might buy it, but she doesn't have enough money yet," said Meredith. "Then she wouldn't have to put up with Frank and his mean attitude."

Mary walked in the restaurant and walked over to the table with the kids.

"It's just about time for you boys to leave," said Mary. "You get to fly on the Beaver."

"A beaver? I was hoping to fly on a plane!" exclaimed Michael.

Meredith started laughing and grabbed at her stomach. "The BEAVER is a kind of plane! It's a de Havilland Beaver!"

Michael blushed a little and shrugged his shoulders.

Johnny shook his head.

Luke stated, "That's our Michael!"

CHAPTER SIX

The boys climbed into the front of the loaded Beaver and their dads climbed in the back. Luke sat next to the pilot, with Johnny and Michael in the next row.

"I've got three extra headsets for you boys if you want to listen or talk to me," said the pilot.

He made sure everyone was buckled in and closed the door. The men on the dock pushed the plane out a little and the pilot started the engine. He pulled some levers and pushed some buttons and the propeller turned faster. Soon the plane was moving on the water, heading toward one end of the lake.

"I'm moving to this side of the lake so we can take off into the wind," the pilot explained.

The boys nodded in understanding as they looked out of their windows. The pilot reached down and pulled another lever. He then reached forward and slowly increased power to the engine. The plane bounced a little on the waves of the lake. Then the large floats on either side of the plane started to level off and slowly separated from the water as the plane took off. They slowly gained altitude and speed until the lake disappeared from view.

Johnny adjusted his microphone and said, "That was the coolest thing ever!"

The pilot smiled and gave him the thumbs up. "I thought you guys would like it. There is nothing like flying a small plane like this, and we have a perfect day for it."

The sky was a beautiful blue and there wasn't a cloud in sight. On the ground below they could see lake after lake followed by forests of trees.

"Look down there," the pilot said through his microphone. "See that open area? That's where some logging was done. It's one of our biggest industries up here."

"Will we see any animals from up here?" said Luke.

"Sometimes, so keep a lookout," said the pilot.

Just then the pilot moved the controls on the plane to send it downward a little. He pointed at a marsh next to a lake.

"There is a moose down there," he said. "See it?"

The boys nodded, pressing their faces on the windows of the plane.

The forty-five minute plane ride went by very fast with the pilot pointing out a few more moose and even a bear. He started adjusted the levers and buttons again, and the plane started moving downward toward a lake.

"There it is – Pelican Lake," said the pilot. "It's one of the best fishing lakes around!"

The plane dropped down even further and it seemed as if it was barely going to miss some trees when the lake quickly appeared beneath them. The pilot then touched the floats of the plane down onto the water into a very smooth landing. The plane taxied along the water toward a very large dock where a man stood waiting. When the plane was about fifty feet away, the pilot turned off the engine, turned the plane a bit, and coasted into the dock. The man grabbed a rope hanging from the plane and tied it to the dock.

"Welcome to Stormy's Fish Camp," the man said as he opened the door. "I'm the caretaker here. They call me Ole Tom."

The boys shook Ole Tom's hand and introduced themselves as he helped them off the plane.

"How was the plane ride?" he asked.

"It was awesome!" exclaimed Michael. "We saw moose and bears and logging areas and a billion lakes."

"Well, you landed on the best one!" said Ole Tom. "Meredith called us from the office and said to take good care of you guys."

The boys knew they were going to like Ole Tom. He had lots of wrinkles and his hair was thinning, but his skin was a golden tan from the sun. There was a twinkle in his eyes when he smiled.

He put his arms around the boys and said, "Let's go show you around camp and find you your cabin."

The camp was situated on a peninsula of an island. On the end of the peninsula was the dock for the airplanes. On either side of the peninsula were two bays of water, each with a large dock holding a number of boats. Three cabins stood by each bay.

"Ok, right up here is the main island cabin. That's where I stay. If you need anything, that's where I'll be," said Ole Tom. "To the left is what we call Grass Bay and to the right is Fish Bay."

"I think I want to stay in Fish bay," said Johnny hopefully.

"Then Fish Bay it is!" exclaimed Ole Tom. "One of our cabins had a water leak so I am going to have you guys stay in Stormy's old cabin. No one has stayed in there for years, but it's the best looking cabin in Ontario."

"How come no one stays in it?" asked Luke.

"I guess I have just felt a little funny about people staying in it since Stormy's disappearance, but I think it's time that people get to enjoy the place," said Ole Tom. "Meredith also told me she told you guys the story about Stormy. I know he would have loved to have you stay there."

Ole Tom showed the boys the fish house where they cleaned the fish and the storage area and walked them down the rock path to Stormy's cabin.

"Forty-four!" said Luke.

"What was that?" said Ole Tom.

"Oh, I was just counting the rock steps from the dock to the cabin," said Luke. "There are forty-four of them."

"Never knew that," said Ole Tom. "Well, go in and look around boys. I'll go help your dads with the gear."

The boys walked into Stormy's old cabin and were amazed at the beauty of the inside. There was a kitchen on one end and a bunch of couches on the other. The couches were situated around a very large stone fireplace. The view of the lake through the large windows was amazing. The cabin had two bedrooms, one with a triple bunk bed. When the boys saw the bunk, a war of rock, paper, and scissors began until Michael earned the top bunk.

"This place is so cool," said Johnny. "Let's go help with the gear so we can fish sooner."

The three boys took off down the steps, each trying to be the first one down to the dock.

CHAPTER SEVEN

The boat was made of aluminum with a twenty-five horsepower motor. Johnny's dad started it up and began to drive it out into the lake. Luke and his dad were in the next boat, followed by Michael and his dad. The lake was smooth like glass and the boats cut a nice path through the water. Ole Tom had told the dads where to fish and filled their buckets with minnows. After about ten minutes, the three boats came to a stop near each other and the fishermen dropped their anchors.

"The hook with the weight on it is called a jig. Tie it to your line and put a minnow on it," said Johnny's dad.

"Do I drop the line down now?" Johnny asked.

"Yep, drop it to the bottom and then lift the line up about six inches and move it up and down a little. That's what they call jigging," explained his dad.

Johnny moved the line up and down by raising and lowering the tip of his fishing rod. After a couple of minutes the tip of the rod jerked downward.

"Set the hook!" Johnny's dad yelled.

Johnny lifted the rod up quickly and the rod bent over toward the water.

"I got one!" screamed Johnny. "Hey Luke, Hey Michael, I got one!"

Luke and Michael were laughing out loud.

"Hey Johnny, we are only twenty feet away! We can hear you just fine," laughed Luke.

Johnny reeled in and his dad grabbed the net. Johnny lifted the end of his rod toward his dad, who scooped the fish into the net.

"Nice walleye, Johnny!" he said. "It's the perfect size to eat!"

Just then Michael stood up and screamed, "I got one."

"I got one too," Luke yelled at the top of his lungs.

Johnny turned toward the other boys, "Hey guys, I can hear you just fine too!"

Everyone laughed and reeled in their fish. The spot was full of fish and they just kept biting. After a couple hours, a bald eagle swooped down and picked up a dead fish not too far from the boats. Everyone stopped to watch the eagle carry the fish in its talons up to its nest at the top of an old evergreen tree. A lot of screeching in the nest came from the three baby eagles that each wanted a share of the food.

"I think that's our sign," said Michael's dad. "It's time for us to go back and eat some of our fish."

"I think that's a great idea," answered Johnny's dad as he started up his boat.

After the short ride, the boys ran up to the main cabin to find Ole Tom. Each of them held walleyes on a stringer, trying to keep them from hitting the ground. Ole Tom walked out of the cabin, smiling from ear to ear.

"That's a mighty fine bunch of walleyes you boys have there," he said. "I think we should head over to the fish house and fillet those. They will make a great supper for all of you."

Ole Tom grabbed the stringers and headed into the fish house. He skillfully cut through the walleyes and removed the fillets. The dads walked in and watched Ole Tom as he cleaned each piece of fish carefully.

"Care to join the boys and us for some walleye, Ole Tom?" said Luke's dad.

"There is nothing I'd like better," he replied.

CHAPTER EIGHT

Johnny's dad dipped the fish fillets into the batter and handed them to Michael's dad at the stove. He dropped them into the hot oil where they cooked to a golden brown. Everyone got a plate of fried fish, French fries, and corn.

"I'm starving," said Michael. "I could eat a horse."

"Hey Michael, why don't you try the fish instead!" Johnny laughed.

Michael dug into his food first and, judging by the look on his face, the walleye was delicious. Everyone was nodding approval.

"There is nothing like fresh walleye," stated Ole Tom.

"I totally agree," replied Johnny's dad.

"Ole Tom, did you know Stormy?" asked Johnny.

"I sure did," he replied. "He was one of the best fishermen in the north woods. He knew every inch of this lake."

"If he knew the lake so well, how did he die?" asked Luke.

"You know, Luke, that's something I've asked myself a lot," said Ole Tom. "It's quite a mystery to me how he was never found. When Frank came back and told everyone that Stormy was lost in some bad weather, the Royal Canadian Mounties flew up here and looked for three days. They never found any sign of him or his boat. Finally, the Mounties called off the search."

"That doesn't make sense," said Michael.

"Meredith said he was a great outdoorsman. Why would he go fishing in bad weather? " asked Johnny.

"We will probably never know the answer to that question," said Ole Tom.

He reached to the center of the table and put another piece of walleye on his plate.

"You boys would have loved Stormy. He really loved to show kids how to fish," he said. "His spirit is still here at the fish camp, though."

"What do you mean?" asked Michael.

"Well, I know this sounds weird, but I sometimes think I hear him in the wind or see his reflection on the lake," said Ole Tom. "He loved this lake so much, I bet he would never leave."

Luke's eyes were getting wider. He was known not to be fond of scary stories.

"You mean like a g-g-ghost or something?" he asked.

"No, nothing like that Luke," said Ole Tom. "I just mean that I sometimes feel he is trying to tell me something . . . but I don't know what."

"So what's the weather going to be like tomorrow?" Luke asked quickly.

Everyone in the room laughed; they could tell that Luke was trying to change the subject away from any stories of ghosts or spirits.

"How about we clean up and make a fire," said Johnny's dad, trying to help Luke.

"I'll see you all later," said Ole Tom. "Remember, we turn the generators off at ten-thirty at night, so there is no power after that. Good night!"

CHAPTER NINE

The fire was slowly burning down to small coals, and the boys had tired of poking into it with sticks. The room was lit from the dim glow of the fire and the moon coming in through the windows.

"I think I've got a stomach ache," Michael said from the couch.

"Do you think it was the seven s'mores you ate?" Luke chuckled.

"Eight!" Johnny corrected Luke. "It could be the four pieces of walleye that he ate too!"

Everyone was tucked into the couches and chairs, and the room was warm from the fire.

"OK boys, I think it's time to head off for bed. It's going to be a long day tomorrow so you'd better get some sleep," said Johnny's dad.

Without any complaint, the boys headed off to the bunk beds. Each of the beds was covered with a thick down comforter and had a soft feather pillow at the top.

"What a great day!" said Johnny. "This place is awesome!"

"This cabin is really sweet too," stated Michael.

"And Ole Tom is really nice. What do you think about the spirit stuff?" asked Luke.

"You are such a worry wart," said Johnny.

Michael climbed to the top bunk and dove under the covers.

"No, really!" Luke went on. "Do you think he is serious?"

"Of course not!" said Johnny.

Suddenly he gasped and pointed behind where Luke was standing. His mouth dropped open and he let out a scream.

"Behind you, Luke! A ghost!" he yelled.

Luke's eyes were the size of pancakes, and he whipped his head around to look where Johnny was pointing.

"Where?" he screamed, jumping backward.

Johnny and Michael started laughing uncontrollably. Luke sneered back at them after he figured out it was a trick.

"Not funny!" he said. "Not Funny!"

Johnny hopped into the second bunk as he wiped the tears of laughter from his eyes.

"Just turn off the light, Luke," Johnny said. "There is no such thing as ghosts or spirits."

Luke closed the door and turned off the light. As quick as he could, he threw himself into his bunk and under the covers. Michael and Johnny were still quietly snickering in the bunks when the light in the room came back on.

"Luke, turn off the light!" said Michael. "Let's get some sleep."

"I did," Luke said as he got out of bed.

He flicked the light off and jumped back into bed. Quite a few minutes went by and the boys were almost asleep when the light came on again.

"It wasn't me," said Luke.

"I'll turn it off," Johnny said, jumping from the bed.

Johnny turned off the switch and got back into bed. A few seconds later the light in the room began to flicker a bit. Michael leaned over the top bunk and looked at Johnny and Luke.

"That's really weird," he said.

"I think it's Stormy playing with the lights!" exclaimed Luke.

"That's silly!" answered Michael.

The light continued to barely flicker on and off.

"What time is it, Michael?" asked Johnny.

Michael looked at his watch and leaned over the bed.

"It's after eleven," he said. "Why?"

"Didn't Ole Tom say the generator was shut off at ten-thirty?" Johnny asked.

"Yeah, so what?" said Michael.

"Well, if there is no generator to power the lights after ten-thirty and it's eleven now . . . . . " said Johnny.

"No such thing as ghosts or spirits, huh?" said Luke shakily.

Immediately the light turned off and the room went black. The boys could hear each other pull their covers over their heads. Not another word was said.

CHAPTER TEN

"I swear the lights kept coming on and off and it was past eleven o'clock!" Michael explained.

The boys had run down to the main cabin immediately after they got up to tell Ole Tom about the lights.

"First the light came back on and then we turned it off and then it came on again," explained Johnny.

"Then the light came back on and it flickered for a long time," added Luke.

"Now, now boys. I'm sure there is an explanation," Ole Tom said. "Maybe there was still some electricity in the lines or something."

Ole Tom scratched his head a little and continued.

"Maybe I turned the generator off a little late last night," he added. "The older I get, the more forgetful I become."

The boys nodded in agreement.

"Why don't you boys try casting off the dock for some northern pike," Ole Tom said. "Try a spinner blade or a spoon lure. Make sure and let the lure sink close to the bottom; the pike like the deeper, colder water."

Johnny, Michael, and Luke ran down toward their cabin to grab their fishing rods.

Ole Tom walked down a little toward the lake and scratched his head again.

"Alright Stormy, what are you up to?" he said quietly.

CHAPTER ELEVEN

The boys were casting their lures out into the water, hoping to catch a northern pike. After a while, the casting became a competition to see who could throw the lures the farthest. Johnny threw his as far as he could and let his spoon sink to the bottom while he waited for the other two to cast.

"Hey guys, I got something," he yelled.

Johnny started reeling until the tension in the line bent the pole.

"I think you are snagged," said Michael.

Johnny pulled a little harder and reeled in a little more.

"I think it's moving, but not very much," he said. "I don't think it's a fish, though. It feels like it's dragging across the bottom. A fish would be fighting back."

Johnny pulled up on his rod and kept reeling. Slowly but surely, whatever he had snagged was coming in closer to the dock. Finally it was below them, and Johnny lifted it up slowly with his rod.

"It's a tackle box!" exclaimed Luke.

Michael reached down into the water and lifted the box onto the dock. It was kind of a green color from the algae that covered its surface. Luke ran over to the nearest boat, grabbed an old towel, and began to wipe down the tackle box. The metal box was old and rusty from the water. It had a nameplate with engraved initials on the top.

"Does it say anything?" asked Johnny.

Luke scrubbed the name plate again.

"It's a bit hard to read, but I think the initials read S.W." said Michael.

Luke stood up and stated quickly, "It's Stormy's tackle box. S.W. – Stormy Weathers."

"Open it up!" said Johnny. "Let's see what's inside!"

Michael carefully lifted the latch on the outside of the tackle box and pried open the lid. The hinges were rusty, so it took a little effort to get it open all the way. Michael tipped the box over after he got it open and drained out most of the water. The inside was full of very old lures. One by one, the boys laid them out on the dock to inspect them.

"I wonder how many fish these have caught?" asked Johnny.

"I don't know, but they look really old!" said Luke.

The boys separated them into spoon and plugs. The plugs were lures that were made mostly of wood and painted, usually red and white. Most of the hooks were rusty but the lures, for the most part, were in pretty good shape.

"Hey what's this?" asked Michael.

"It's an old key!" exclaimed Johnny. "I wonder what it's for?"

"I bet Ole Tom will know!" answered Luke excitedly.

The boys scrambled to put the lures back into the tackle box and made their way up the rock steps to the main cabin.

"Ole Tom!" they yelled in unison.

Ole Tom came out, wiping some grease off his hands with a towel.

"What's up boys?" he asked.

"We found Stormy's tackle box!" they exclaimed.

"Well, let's have a look see," he said.

He looked at the box and the initials and opened the tackle box again. He dug through the contents of the box until Michael interrupted him.

"And we found this too!" Michael said as he showed him the old key.

Ole Tom took the key from Michael and held it up a little to get a better look. Then he wiped the key off with his shirt.

Finally he said, "Amazing."

"What do you mean – amazing?" asked Johnny.

"I think you boys are right," stated Ole Tom. "I think this is Stormy's old tackle box. I can't believe you found it."

"We caught it casting off the dock. I snagged it with my lure," said Johnny.

"Off the dock? Guests have cast off the dock for years," said Ole Tom. "You would have thought it would have been dragged in by now."

He stood up and started walking out the door of the main cabin, the boys hurrying after him.

"And I think I know what this key is for," he added.

Ole Tom walked into the storage shed where most of the tools were kept. Life preservers, fish stringers, and minnow buckets hung from the rafters and walls. Old boat motors, partially assembled and in a state of repair, were scattered in the middle. Ole Tom walked to the back of the shed and moved some boxes out of the way as he stepped over an old motor. When he got to the very back, he began to rummage through some older wooden crates. He fumbled around for a while and slowly lifted a small box from the bottom of one crate.

"Here it is!" said Ole Tom. "I threw this in this crate years ago because I didn't know what it was or who it belonged to and didn't have the key. I completely forgot it until now."

Ole Tom gave the key to Luke, who slowly slid it into the keyhole. He gave the key a turn to the right and the box clicked open. Luke opened the box and pulled out a small rolled up piece of paper. He spread it out over a piece of wood.

"It looks like a map, I think," said Johnny.

"But where?" said Michael.

"Well, I think it is Strawberry Island," stated Ole Tom. "It's an island that looks like a strawberry on the far end of the lake, a place that Stormy used to fish a lot."

"What do you think it means?" asked Johnny.

"I can't say for sure but I would guess it's just a location of a fishing spot," answered Ole Tom. "And the 'X' is probably where he used to put his boat or where he cast out from shore."

Michael picked up the map while Luke was examining the box and key.

"I think we should clean up the box and lures and give them to Meredith. I bet she would like to have them," said Johnny.

"That's a great idea, boys. I'm sure she would," replied Ole Tom.

The three boys headed off to the cabin with the new found treasures.

Ole Tom watched as the boys ran off and muttered to himself, "Ok Stormy, first the lights, now your tackle box. What are you up to?"

CHAPTER TWELVE

"**C**an we go fish Strawberry Island? Please!" Johnny pleaded with his dad. "It's where Stormy used to fish. It's got to be awesome."

"I don't see why not," answered Johnny's dad.

Luke and Michael's dads agreed and they all headed out toward the boats. The ride took about forty-five minutes, but the sights were amazing. In one spot Luke's dad pointed out a beaver dam and a large number of trees that were chewed at the bases. They finally arrived at the group of islands on the map.

"It's that one over there," said Johnny, pointing to the island in the middle. "Can you drop us off? We want to fish from shore."

"I suppose so," replied Johnny's dad. "We will fish close by, near one of the other islands. Just yell when you want us to pick you up."

The boys were dropped off on the island and they carried their rods onto shore. Strawberry Island wasn't that big, but it was larger than they'd imagined from the map.

"Let's look around," said Michael.

Luke picked up a large stick and broke off the smaller branches.

"What's that for?" asked Johnny.

"I guess to protect myself," Luke replied.

"From a ghost?" Michael chuckled. "I don't think a stick will keep a ghost away."

"Well, it makes me feel safer anyway," said Luke.

The boys were at the north part of the island and started walking to where the "X" was located on the south end. There weren't too many trees on the island and they reached the other end in just a couple of minutes. Johnny was in front and stopped all of a sudden.

"Hey guys, help me brush the leaves away," he said. "I think I stepped on something."

The boys crouched down and began to clear the leaves from what they exposed as a very large, flat rock. Johnny dug his fingers down around the rock about an inch or so.

"It's not very thick," he said. "Let's try to lift it."

The three of them all got on one side of the rock and dug their fingers underneath the thin rock. They tried to lift it, but it wouldn't budge.

"I've got an idea," said Luke.

He ran over to the shoreline and picked up a small boulder about six inches high. Luke placed the small boulder next to the flat rock, then took the stick he was carrying, and pushed it into the ground where his fingers had dug. The stick acted as a lever against the rock, and slowly he began to pry the flat rock from the ground. Seeing the rock move, Johnny and Michael helped to lift the flat rock off the ground until it opened like a door and finally came to rest against a tree.

"Holy Moly!" said Johnny. "It's a bunch of bones and a skull!"

Luke, despite being plenty scared, reached down and grabbed a small chain from below the skull. Attached to the chain was a small medal with a picture of a saint or something. Luke turned it over and read the inscription.

"It says 'With Love, Mary' on the back," he said.

"Mary is Stormy's daughter. This is Stormy Weathers!" Michael gasped.

Johnny was still crouched down, looking very closely at the skull. He moved to the other side of the skull and looked even closer.

"Look on that side of the skull over there. There is a hole." Johnny stated. "And on this side is another hole with a bullet still in it!"

The three boys looked closely at the skull for a while before they all decided it was time to go. They carefully lowered the flat rock down on top of Stormy's bones and made their way back to the other end of the island. The boats weren't far offshore and the dads promptly came and picked them up. After another boat ride, the boys hopped out onto the dock and ran up toward the main cabin.

CHAPTER THIRTEEN

Luke handed the medal to Ole Tom. The boys told him the story of the flat rock and how they had pried it off the ground. They described the bullet hole and the bullet still lodged in the side of the skull.

"So someone killed Stormy," said Ole Tom. "That comes as quite a shock to me. Stormy was liked by everyone."

The boys and Ole Tom talked about the chain and the skull and the grave for quite a while until finally Ole Tom stood up.

"Well there is nothing we can do now," he said. "I suggest we forget about it for now until the plane comes to get you and you can tell Frank to send someone out to investigate. I also suggest that we have a fishing tournament to forget about this," he added. "It's time to have some fun."

Ole Tom walked down the rock steps to the dock where the three boys' dads were waiting to go fishing.

"We are going to have a fishing tournament this afternoon," he stated. "All walleyes will be measured by weight and all northern pike will be measured in inches. The winner gets a trophy and also gets to pick what flavor of home-made ice cream we make tonight."

Ole Tom paused to lick his lips. He brought his hand to his face and whispered "My favorite is vanilla."

"How much time do we have?" asked Johnny.

"You have three hours . . . now get going!" Ole Tom said with a smile.

The boys and their dads loaded into their boats and headed in three different directions.

"So you finally wanted to be found, eh Stormy?" muttered Ole Tom.

CHAPTER FOURTEEN

Dinner that night was in the main cabin and Ole Tom was serving steaks, tater tots and green beans. There wasn't much talking going on as everyone was busy stuffing his face with food. The steak was delicious and they had all worked up an appetite from the fishing contest.

"Ok everyone, one at a time I want you boys to stand up and tell me what size walleye you caught today," said Ole Tom.

Johnny stood up first and quickly announced "I caught a four pound, four ounce walleye."

Luke stood up next and stated "Me too, mine was four pounds and four ounces."

"Four pounds, four ounces for me. Wow, we were exactly the same!" exclaimed Michael.

Ole Tom rubbed his chin and laughed at the coincidence. "All right then, how about the northern pike?"

Luke jumped in first this time. "I caught a lunker. He was forty-four inches!"

"Me too!" Johnny and Michael screamed at the same time.

Everyone shook their heads in amazement.

Johnny, Luke, and Michael walked over to each other. They all made fists and touched them together. "Knuckles!" they yelled.

"Well, I've never seen anything like it," said Ole Tom. "I guess it's officially a tie and since no one won, I'll just have to pick vanilla for the home-made ice cream tonight!"

The boys cleared the table and Ole Tom poured the ingredients into the old wooden ice cream maker. The dads went outside to build a bonfire. Each of the boys took a turn winding the ice cream maker. After about an hour the ice cream was ready, and everyone took a bowl to his seat by the fire. The conversation quickly turned back to the tackle box, the key, the map, and the grave. No one had an idea how Stormy had been killed. Ole Tom stood up and announced he was heading off to bed.

"The plane will be here early tomorrow so have all your gear packed early," he said.

The boys headed off to the cabin. Luke and Michael jumped into bed while Johnny was in the main room. Johnny walked into the room, and something was obviously on his mind.

"What's going on, Johnny," asked Luke.

"I think Stormy is trying to tell us something," said Johnny.

"What do you mean by that," said Michael.

"I just counted the number of windows in the cabin and there are eleven," Johnny said.

"So?" said Michael.

"Each window has four panes in it. Eleven times four is forty-four," he said.

"Ok, and that means what?" said Luke.

"Well Luke, how many rocks are on the stone path?" Johnny asked.

"Umm, forty-four, right?" answered Luke.

"And how much did our walleyes weigh?" Johnny continued.

"Four pounds four ounces," Luke and Michael answered together.

"I think I get it now, Stormy IS trying to tell us something," Luke said. "How many inches long were our northern pike?"

Michael still looked puzzled. "Forty-four inches."

"Well let me walk you through it then," said Johnny. "Forty-four rocks, forty-four window panes, four pound, four ounce walleyes and forty-four inch northerns. Stormy was killed by a bullet that came from a . . . . ."

" A forty-four," said Luke. "A Colt .44"

"And who do we know that owns a Colt .44?" asked Johnny.

Michael answered quietly, "Frank, that's who. Mean old Frank."

The boys jumped into bed knowing what they had to do.

CHAPTER FIFTEEN

"I hope you boys have a safe flight back," said Ole Tom.

The boys took turns giving Ole Tom hugs and climbed into the plane.

"I'll miss you boys!" he said.

The plane ride seemed to take forever. By the time they landed on the lake near the office it was still early in the morning. Meredith was waiting on the dock for the boys. As soon as the door opened, the three boys jumped off the plane.

"Follow us!" they yelled to Meredith as they raced past her.

"Where are we going?" she asked as she took off after them.

"To the restaurant to find Bill," Johnny answered.

"You know, the Royal Canadian Mountie," said Michael.

The boys ran into the restaurant and told Bill and Meredith the entire story. They gave the medal with the inscription to him and told them their theory of how Stormy was killed. Bill listened carefully to every word and even took some notes on a pad. Meredith listened carefully as well and was shocked when the boys told her who they thought had killed her grandfather.

Bill thanked the boys and promised to check out their story right away. Johnny's dad walked into the restaurant and announced it was time to leave. The boys gave Meredith the tackle box and map and then went outside and loaded themselves into the car. Meredith was waving to the boys when her mom, Mary, walked up next to her. As the car left the parking lot, they could see Meredith telling her mom the story the boys had just told Bill of the Royal Canadian Mounted Police. Mary raised her hand to her mouth and looked back at the office just as the car passed out of view.

CHAPTER SIXTEEN

A few days had passed and the boys were already back into their routine of baseball and James Bond movies. They were lying on the bunk bed of the fort when a knocking sound came from the door.

"Grand slam," said Johnny's dad.

Johnny stuck out his head of the window.

"That was the password last week, Dad," said Johnny. "This time 'hat trick' is the password."

"Well, get the other boys and come down here," his dad said.

The boys climbed out of the fort and stood around him.

"I just got a call from Mary Weathers. She said that Frank confessed to killing Stormy all those years ago," said Johnny's dad. "Apparently he killed him in order to get the business all for himself."

Johnny's dad went on. "They checked the bullet from the skull to Frank's Colt .44, and it was a match."

"What's going to happen to Mary and Meredith?" asked Johnny.

"Well, that's exactly what Mary called about. Frank forged Stormy's signature on a phony agreement. So that means that the new owners of Stormy's Fish Camp are Mary and Meredith," Johnny's dad said.

"That's great!" said Michael.

"There's more!" said Johnny's dad. "In appreciation for all that you did for them, Mary and Meredith have invited us all back next year as their guests."

"Awesome," said Johnny. "I can't wait for next year already."

The boys climbed back into the fort and crawled onto the bed.

"We wouldn't have figured it out without Stormy's help," said Luke.

"You're right, Luke. I believe in spirits now!" said Michael.

"I'm really happy for Mary and Meredith. I think Stormy was tired of Frank treating them so poorly," said Johnny. "I don't think things could have turned out any better."

Johnny stuck out his fist. Michael and Luke did the same.

All together the boys said "Knuckles!"

The Skateboard King

To Johnny, Luke, and Michael

My son and his two best friends

CHAPTER ONE

"Ready! Break!" exclaimed the boys as they moved toward the line of scrimmage. Michael put his hands underneath the center and looked to his right and then to his left. Johnny was lined up on the right in the slot back position and Luke was lined up behind Michael. Coach Krowley was crouched on the sideline with his list of plays rolled up in his hands. He was looking at the scoreboard that showed just four seconds remaining in the first half. The boys played for Mapleville Tire Center and so far had endured a terrible half. Dumont Construction was leading 21 to 0. Scottie Dumont, their leading rusher, had scored three touchdowns on very long runs. Both teams had won their first two games very easily and expected this game to be difficult, but so far it was all Dumont Construction.

"Blue 32!" yelled Michael. "Blue 32, Hut! Hut!"

The center, Joey Spinelli, hiked the ball to Michael. Luke started to move toward the line of scrimmage to Michael's left. Michael reached out to hand off the ball and at the last second pulled it away on a fake. Johnny was running toward the middle of the field and at the same time as the fake he cut to the right, heading for the sideline.

Luke ducked his head and crashed into the line, hoping to make the linebackers stay in the middle of the field. When the Dumont Construction team realized it was a fake, many of them yelled "Pass!" Michael spun and rolled to the right and started in that direction. His eyes were focused downfield and he spotted Johnny moving quickly to the right. Johnny had his left hand extended in the air, indicating he was open.

Michael stopped quickly and planted his feet. He raised the ball up by his ear and fired the football into the air. Just as he released the ball, the linebacker for Dumont Construction pummeled him backward and drove him to the ground.

The cornerback covering Johnny was still behind him by two steps as Johnny leaped into the air. At the five yard line he stretched out his arms and grabbed the ball. He tucked the ball away and stopped abruptly. The cornerback was moving so fast that Johnny's quick stop caused him to misjudge his tackle. Johnny pushed him toward the sideline and darted down the sideline into the end zone.

Luke was screaming as he patted Johnny on the helmet. The team surrounded and congratulated Johnny, who made his way out of the group and looked back toward the line of scrimmage for Michael. Michael was still on the ground with his hands stretched in the air signaling a touchdown.

Johnny ran toward him and reached down to help him up.

"Nice pass!" he said as he made a fist and held it out toward Michael.

Nice catch!" replied Michael.

Luke ran up to the other two boys and they all touched fists together.

"Knuckles," they said and they ran off for halftime.

CHAPTER TWO

The Mapleville Tire Center football team gathered around Coach Krowley, waiting for him to explode about how poorly they had played so far. Instead Coach Krowley was calm and quiet as he started to speak.

"We ended the half on a good note, boys," he said. "I'm glad we finally started to make some plays."

"However," he continued, "we must stop Scottie Dumont. He is running right through us."

"How are we going to do that?" asked Joey Spinelli.

"Good question, Joey!" answered Coach Krowley. "I think we will switch our defense and play a five man front with three linebackers. I hope that will make our line harder to get through. Johnny and Luke, I want you two to switch from cornerbacks on defense to linebackers. That should give us speed in the middle as well. Danny J and Danny R will be playing cornerbacks. Ryan will keep playing safety. We need to plug up the middle."

"If we think they might pass," he continued, "I'll tap my head and signal for Johnny and Luke to switch back to cornerback."

The entire team was nodding in agreement, knowing that Coach Krowley's adjustments would help.

"We get the ball first so we need to score to get back in the game," he said. "I think we might try the old hook and ladder play."

Coach Krowley motioned for the offensive backfield to come closer and he drew the play on his erasable clipboard. When he was finished, the boys all put their hands towards each other in the middle and raised them in the air.

Michael, who was the captain of the team, started by yelling "Mapleville Tire Center!"

"M – T – C!" the team yelled loudly in unison.

With that the boys ran out on the field energized and ready to start the second half.

CHAPTER THREE

Dumont Construction kicked off and Johnny darted and weaved and ran the ball to the thirty-five yard line.

Danny R ran into the huddle and told Michael the play.

"Hook and ladder on one," said Michael. "Make sure the defensive end doesn't get to me."

The boys broke from the huddle and lined up in the same formation as the last play of the first half. Johnny was off to the right and Luke was behind Michael except a little to his right. Michael walked up the line and Joey hiked the ball.

The lines crashed into each other and Michael and Luke headed to the right. Johnny headed straight downfield. The cornerback covering him was giving plenty of room so he wouldn't get beat again. Michael was getting ready to throw again and Luke broke downfield to the right of Johnny.

Johnny stopped and turned around about fifteen yards downfield. Michael had already thrown the ball quickly and it headed just above Johnny's head. The cornerback saw the ball coming and moved toward him. Just as Johnny caught the ball he flicked it to his left to Luke who was streaking down the sideline. The cornerback couldn't recover or change directions quickly enough to even put a hand on Luke.

Luke bolted down another fifty yards untouched and tossed the ball to the referee after he crossed the goal line. Luke ran back to the sideline and high-fived Coach Krowley.

"Nice call, Coach!" he exclaimed.

"Kickoff team," said Coach Krowley as he motioned for the players to get on the field.

Michael kicked off to Scottie Dumont and Scottie returned the ball to the forty yard line.

The Mapleville Tire Center defense headed onto the field and Johnny and Luke took their new positions as linebackers.

Dumont Construction tried to run the same kinds of plays up the middle that they had in the first half. They didn't have as much luck, though, as more Mapleville boys on the line and more speed at linebacker seemed to stop their attack. Coach Krowley even had Ryan do a safety blitz right up the middle and he tackled Scottie Dumont for a loss of five yards. Dumont Construction had to punt after only one first down and it became Mapleville Tire Center's chance with the ball.

Coach Krowley tried all kinds of plays and formations. He tried Johnny and Luke in the backfield in the wishbone formation and tried to sweep and option to the sides. He tried a power I formation with Luke behind Michael and Johnny behind Luke. Nothing they tried worked. They even tried the hook and ladder again, but the safety for Dumont Construction read the play and broke it up. With about two minutes to go in the game, Dumont Construction had the ball and was trying to run out the clock since they were ahead 21 to 14.

The boys for Mapleville Tire Center were stopping Dumont's running game, but were running out of time. They had stopped the first two rushes and left Dumont Construction with a third down and eight yards to go. Coach Krowley yelled to get Michael's attention. He was tapping his head quickly.

"Watch the pass!" Coach yelled.

Michael nodded and tapped his head in the direction of Johnny and Luke. The two boys switched from linebackers to cornerbacks.

Dumont Construction hiked the ball and Scottie Dumont went for the handoff. The quarterback faked the ball and, just as Coach Krowley had predicted, he dropped back for a pass. The quarterback threw the ball far downfield toward his wide receiver. Johnny was covering the pass and quickly closed on the receiver. He leaped in the air as the pass came down and tipped it away toward the middle of the field.

Ryan was behind them and intercepted the ball before it hit the ground. He started to run, then slowed down a little waiting for Johnny to catch up. Johnny got in front of Ryan and knocked down the first opposing player he saw. Michael moved in Ryan's direction and hit one of the Dumont Construction players into another one and made a path for Ryan. He continued to run until he was finally brought down at the three yard line.

Coach Krowley couldn't stop the clock as he was out of time outs. It took three plays, but Michael finally scored on a quarterback sneak with only eleven seconds left. Michael kicked the extra point to tie the game 21 to 21.

Everyone ran to the sideline huddle with a lot of excitement.

Danny R high-fived Danny J and yelled, "Overtime!"

CHAPTER FOUR

"**N**ot so fast," said Coach Krowley. "We need to play smart. Let's not allow them to run this one back."

The kickoff team ran out to the middle of the field to the huddle. Michael placed the ball on the tee and walked back to the huddle.

"We have to get down the field a lot faster and pin them deep," said Michael. "Hustle down there and let's make a tackle."

Johnny headed to the far right and Luke to the far left. When the team was set, Michael dropped his hand and booted the ball high into the air. The Mapleville Tire Center team flew down the field with a new fire in their eyes and knocked over most of the opposing team.

Scottie Dumont was waiting patiently for the ball and caught it on the fifteen yard line. By the time he looked up, he realized that there wasn't much room to maneuver. He started to go to his left and saw Johnny flying in from the outside. Scottie Dumont changed directions and moved to go to the other sideline. Luke had avoided his blocker as well and was coming in hard from Scottie's right. Scottie stopped in his tracks and was clobbered by Luke and Johnny at the same time.

At the instant that they hit him, the ball squirted out of Scottie Dumont's hands. He fell to the ground and leaped for the ball, but it was just out of his reach.

Joey Spinelli, the biggest boy on the team, saw the ball and scooped it up at the ten yard line. Almost in slow motion he started to move toward the end zone. The clock was down to five seconds and Joey was at the five yard line. A hit from behind spun him completely around. Joey regained his balance and took a couple more steps when it seemed like the whole Dumont Construction team tried to tackle him at once. Joey kept driving his legs and carried them two more yards. He fell into the end zone as time ran off the clock.

Mapleville Tire Center had won the game! The whole team surrounded Joey Spinelli and even tried to lift him on their shoulders. The entire team fell into a pile and burst into a fit of laughter at their inability to hoist Joey into the air.

Coach Krowley ran over to the boys and announced, "Now that's what I call football! Let's go shake their hands and congratulate them on a terrific game."

CHAPTER FIVE

Johnny and Luke were crashed in the beanbags and Michael was on the bottom bunk of the bed in the fort in Johnny's backyard. The portable air conditioner that Johnny's grandpa had given them was on full blast. They had just finished one James Bond movie on the DVD player and the next one was starting.

As always when the theme song started, they made their fingers into pretend guns and started shooting each other. However, today's shooting didn't last very long.

"I'm exhausted," yawned Luke. "That game today tired me out!"

"Me too!" replied Johnny.

Michael passed what was left of the cookies to the other boys.

"Here, have another cookie. It always makes me feel better," he laughed.

Luke and Johnny both grabbed a cookie.

"I can't believe school starts in just two days," Johnny said in a depressed voice.

"Me neither," said Michael. "Hey, we have to do something cool for our last day tomorrow."

"I can't do anything," said Luke. "My mom told me I have to watch my brother, Erik."

"You have to babysit him?" asked Johnny.

"No, it's not that. I have to watch him in the skate-board competition tomorrow," answered Luke.

Mapleville had just built a brand new skate park complete with a large half-pipe and a freestyle area with bumps and lots of grind rails.

"Your little brother is an awesome skateboarder, especially since he is only in second grade," stated Johnny.

"I know! He lives on the thing," said Luke. "He even tried to bring it in to church one time. That didn't go over very well with my mom!"

"Why don't you guys come over with your bikes tomorrow and we can all ride to the skateboard park and watch Erik," suggested Johnny. "We can all hang out together then."

"Sounds good to me," replied Michael. "He's fun to watch anyway."

They all agreed it would be a good way to spend the last day of summer vacation. After the long day and the exciting football game, the tired boys fell asleep one by one while watching the second James Bond movie.

CHAPTER SIX

Johnny was waiting in his driveway on his BMX bike as Luke slid his bike sideways to a stop. Michael did a wheelie, dropped the front tire down, and stopped next to Luke.

"Hey Jackson, hey Duke," said Michael.

Johnny had two brown and white Springer Spaniel dogs and they were wagging their tails, waiting for the boys to pet them and scratch their heads. Jackson had more white on his face from gray hair since he was much older.

"Duke is so funny. His whole body wiggles when he wags his tail," said Luke.

Johnny told the dogs to stay and the boys started off down the street on their bikes. Johnny pedaled a few times and stood on the back pegs of his bike. Luke was weaving back and forth, with Michael following close behind.

"Johnny! Johnny!" came a voice from across the street. "Boys, can you come over please?"

"That's Mrs. Dunbar," Johnny explained to Luke and Michael. "She lives by herself since her husband passed away a few years ago."

"Be right there, Mrs. Dunbar!" he yelled.

The boys crossed the street, hopped off their bikes and walked up to Mrs. Dunbar, who was kneeling in her garden.

"Have you seen Miss Betty?" she asked.

Luke leaned over to Johnny and whispered, "Who is Miss Betty?"

"Miss Betty is her cat," Johnny answered in a regular voice.

"I haven't seen her since I let her out last night," Mrs. Dunbar said sadly. "She has never been gone this long before. I'm afraid something has happened to her."

"What does she look like?" asked Michael.

"Well, she is all white," she answered, pausing to wipe a tear from her eye. "She has very long fur and a pink collar."

"I haven't seen her, but we are just going out now," Johnny said. "We will keep an eye out for her."

"Oh goodness, thank you," said Mrs. Dunbar with a little more energy. "I'll make you the biggest batch of brownies if you find her."

"We'll be sure to try. I love brownies," replied Michael.

"You love all food, Michael!" Luke said as he smacked Michael on the arm.

"We'll make a few trips around the neighborhood before we go to the skate park, Mrs. Dunbar," Johnny said. The boys rode down the street looking between houses and under cars. After three trips around the neighborhood with no luck, they turned in the direction of the skate park.

CHAPTER SEVEN

The Mapleville Skate Park was bustling with lots of parents and skaters preparing for the contest to start. The park was surrounded by a few sets of bleachers with a small pavilion to the side. Under the pavilion were a sign-up table for the contestants, a table holding an assortment of trophies for the winners, and a number of booths for t-shirts, skating gear and food vendors.

"There's the ice cream truck. Do you guys want one? My mom gave me some money," said Johnny.

"Of course," replied Michael.

The boys walked to the truck and looked at the choices listed on the side of the truck. They usually chose the cone called the dogface. It had two swirls of soft ice cream that looked like ears and each was dipped in chocolate sprinkles. Two chocolates for eyes and a cherry in the middle made it resemble a dog's face.

"Three dogfaces, please," Johnny said to the guys working the truck.

"Not too much longer and I'm done serving you punks ice cream!" exclaimed Raz.

"Oh, shut up and get them their ice cream," cried out Pete.

Pete and Raz had taken over the ice cream truck this summer when they'd moved to Mapleville from another town. Pete was bigger with a round face and lots of wavy black hair and Raz was really skinny with spiked bleached hair.

"Here's your ice cream. Now go on," whined Raz in his squeaky voice. "I got more customers."

"He can be such a jerk!" quipped Michael softly.

"What was that?" demanded Raz.

"I said you must love your work!" Michael replied as the boys ran away.

The boys hopped onto the bleachers and scanned the park for Luke's brother Erik.

"There he is," Luke said, pointing at the half-pipe.

Erik was on his way up one of the sides of the half-pipe and leaped off his board and landed on the top platform. His board continued to fly up in the air and he grabbed it with his hand. He turned around and saw the boys in the bleachers. He waved a little and started over toward them.

Erik was short, with two very large dimples in his slightly chubby cheeks. His hair was blond like his brother's, but you couldn't tell as he never went anywhere without his skateboard helmet on. The helmet was black and covered with stickers. The loop straps on each side, always unbuckled, hung down. He wore the required elbow and kneepads for the competition, but that wasn't unusual as his mom made him wear them anyway.

Erik climbed up the bleachers and sat down by the boys.

"Hey Erik, you nervous?" asked Michael.

Erik shook his head and spun the wheels on his skateboard.

"Think you will win?" asked Johnny.

Erik shrugged his shoulders and tilted his head a little.

"Are you gonna try your 360 today?" questioned Luke.

"Maybe," answered Erik.

The announcer stated over the speaker system that the competition was about to begin. The contest would be held in two parts. First would be the free-style and second would be the half-pipe competition. Both scores would be added together for an overall winner.

Erik got up and gave the boys a smile and another small wave. He bounded down the bleachers, hopped on his skateboard when he reached the bottom, and pushed his way onto the park.

"He doesn't say much, does he?" said Michael.

"Only around you guys, I guess. I can't get him to keep quiet at home!" Luke laughed.

CHAPTER EIGHT

"Most of the skateboarders are older than Erik," noted Johnny.

"Don't let that fool you. He twists and gets big air better than any of the other kids," replied Luke.

The three judges were seated at a small table under a portable tent. There were about thirty boys and girls in the competition. Erik was standing in a group of other skaters, watching the competition. After about half of the skaters had competed, the announcer called his name. Erik tossed his skateboard out and pushed out into the park.

"Here he goes!" pointed out Johnny. "He has ninety seconds to do his tricks."

Erik started gaining speed as he rode across the park. He rode up one quarter pipe and launched into the air at the top. While he was in the air, Erik grabbed his board in the middle and landed on a wedge on the other side.

"That was an Indy," stated Luke. "That's what they call it when you grab in the middle. There is a nose grab and a tail grab too."

Erik skated a little farther to a wedge, box, and stair combo. The wedge was on one side with a flat box in the middle, and the stairs were on the other side of the box. Down the middle of the stairs was a handrail made of metal. Erik rode up the wedge and continued on the level box part of the combination. Just before he got to the stairs, he squatted into a crouched stance and bounced upward into the air. Amazingly, the board seemed to stay attached to his feet and lifted in the air as well. Erik jumped all six of the steps and finally landed on the ground.

There was some applause from the bleachers and one lady even stood up and screamed, "Awesome!"

Luke ducked his head and rolled his eyes.

"That was my mom," he whispered to Johnny and Michael.

Erik had done a couple of jumps and grabs on a pyramid-looking ramp and was moving toward a rail that was about ten feet long. He popped his board up onto the rail and skidded both sets of wheels along the entire length of the rail.

"That's called a 50-50 grind. The metal parts of the skateboard that hold the wheels are called trucks. When both trucks grind along the rail and you balance your skateboard in a skid it's called a 50-50," explained Luke.

Erik turned around and balanced his board into a wheelie with the nose in the air and then bounced the tail of the board on the ground and quickly jumped his skateboard over a different rail.

"What was that called?" asked Michael.

"That was a manual followed by an Ollie," described Luke.

Erik had about ten seconds left on his time and moved toward the wedge, box, and stair combo again. He rode up the wedge and crouched down when he made it to the box. Erik flipped the board under his feet and landed the middle of his board on the hand-rail. He slid down the handrail and at the bottom he jumped down off the rail and rode away on his board. The buzzer on the timing clock went off, signaling the end of his time.

The judges were busy tabulating their scores and each handed their papers to a volunteer at the score-board. Erik received an average score of 9.1 which meant he was currently in second place. The people in the crowd were clapping at the great job Erik had done.

"Boy, he is good!" exclaimed Johnny.

"That's why the kids in his class call him the Skateboard King," Luke stated proudly.

Erik stayed in second place for the rest of the free-style part of the competition. He had drawn the final spot in the half-pipe and would go last.

Johnny, Michael, and Luke had spent the entire afternoon watching the skateboard competition in the bleachers except for several trips to the food booths.

"I think I've eaten a little too much," said Michael.

"No kidding? Two dogfaces, two cheeseburgers, an order of fries, a hotdog, and three sodas? Why would you think you ate too much?" Johnny chuckled.

"Ha! Ha! Very funny!" said Michael. "Hey Luke, what will Erik do on the half-pipe?"

"He is gonna have to do something pretty good because the kid in first has a total of 18.2 points," commented Johnny.

"Well, if he plays it safe he will most likely ride the pipe and stop with a nose stall or maybe a rock to fakie," said Luke.

"A what?" asked Michael.

"A nose stall, a tail stall, or a rock to fakie," explained Luke. "A nose or tail stall is when you come to a stop on the top of the half pipe with the edge of your board. A rock is when your board teeters on the edge. That's when you come to a stop on the edge of the half pipe on the middle of your board. The fakie part is just the way your feet are on the board when you go back down the half-pipe."

"What will he do if he doesn't play it safe?" asked Johnny.

"If he wants to win he is going to have to get some big air off the end of the half-pipe and maybe even try a 360 degree spin," said Luke.

The announcer called Erik's name and said he was the last rider in the day's competition. The crowd seemed anxious with excitement but quickly became quiet as he started his run.

Erik put his board on the edge of the half-pipe and stepped on his board. His back foot was pressing down hard on the board, which suspended the rest of it into the air. He adjusted his helmet and then pushed down on his front foot. Erik and his board dropped in on the half-pipe. His knees were bent and his hands were off to his sides. As quickly as he descended, Erik started moving up the other side of the pipe. He made a few trips back and forth, trying to gain some speed.

"I think he will try something here," said Luke.

Erik stopped in a nose stall and then dropped back in on the half-pipe. On his way up the other side he spun his board and then he did a rock to fakie and returned to do a tail stall.

"He's not gonna win this way," said Michael. "He's not going to get enough points."

As he balanced in his tail stall, Erik looked over at the boys as if he had heard Michael. He grinned a little and pressed down on the front of his board. After a couple times back and forth, Erik flew high into the air off the end of the half-pipe.

"Whoa! That was up there!" exclaimed Johnny.

Erik changed directions and came down perfectly onto the pipe. His speed drove him downward very quickly but also pushed him up the other side. When he launched into the air, Erik reached down to grab his board and spun one whole turn before coming down again.

"No way! A frontside 360!" screamed Luke.

Erik landed perfectly again and was crouched down as he rode up the other side. At the top of the half-pipe he reached down again and spun into another whole turn.

"Another one!" yelled Michael and Johnny together.

The three boys were high-fiving each other as Erik ended his run. People were whistling and cheering when the scores were posted. Erik had received a 9.4 for a total of 18.5 and first place!

The announcer was patting Erik on the helmet as he handed him the trophy that was almost as tall as he was. Johnny, Luke, and Michael were cheering wildly and Luke's mom was crying with happiness.

The announcer asked Erik if he had anything to say after his big win and put the microphone in front of him.

Erik got a big grin on his face and both his dimples were showing. His left eyebrow rose a little in a sly sort of way. He leaned over to the microphone and answered, "I wish school didn't start tomorrow."

CHAPTER NINE

The sun was bright and there was a lot of commotion in the parking lot of Holy Spirit School. Coach Krowley, the school gym teacher, was outside watching over the kids playing football, four square, and jump rope. Mrs. Waterman, everyone's favorite kindergarten teacher, was busy exchanging hugs with her former students. Mrs. Greenfield was checking out a tear on a new pair of school pants and a skinned knee underneath. The first bell rang, and all the children made their way through the doors to begin the first day of the new school year.

The boys walked into the sixth grade classroom and looked around to find their desks. All three of them were next to each other. Johnny quickly emptied his backpack of pens, pencils, erasers, and notebooks.

"This is going to be a long year," said Michael.

"Mrs. Crabtree isn't the nicest teacher and she hates recess," added Johnny.

The second bell rang and everyone got into their seats. Mrs. Greenfield, their fifth grade teacher from last year, walked to the front of the class.

"I have an important announcement," she said. "Mrs. Crabtree has decided to retire and I have been moved by the principal to teach sixth grade this year."

Johnny leaned over to Michael and gave him a high-five.

"Awesome," they both screamed.

Mrs. Greenfield gave the boys a stern look. Johnny and Michael slouched back in their desk chairs. Mrs. Greenfield then cracked a smile.

"I'm very happy to have you, too," said Mrs. Greenfield.

The boys loved Mrs. Greenfield because she was a really good teacher and she told the best stories. They even got to call her Mrs. G for short.

"Why don't we begin telling each other what we did on our summer vacation," said Mrs. G.

Some of the children told stories of their trips to Florida and others talked about their camping trips. Mrs. G. described her trip to Italy with her husband. She talked about the food and the amazing history. When she was finished, she paused and got a little choked up.

"Excuse me, class," she said as she tried to regain her composure. "It's just that when we returned home, our poodle ran away."

Mary Beth McDermott, the girl who was always trying to kiss Luke, raised her hand. After Mrs. G called on her, she stood up.

"I'm so sorry, Mrs. G. I know how you feel. We lost our Siamese cat last week. You know, the one that we show in competitions. My mom thinks it ran away, too," said Mary Beth.

Johnny leaned over to Michael, and Luke listened in as well.

"Miss Betty is missing, too," he said. "You know, Mrs. Dunbar's cat."

"That is pretty weird," added Luke. "That's three pets missing."

"Let's get back to your summer vacation experiences," said Mrs. G.

Each of the boys took his turn and told variations of the same story of the fort, football, and hanging out together. When everyone was finished, Mrs. G instructed the class to get out their math books. Summer vacation was officially over.

CHAPTER TEN

Johnny tucked his helmet inside his shoulder pads and shirt. He picked up his helmet by the facemask and grabbed his water bottle with his other hand. Luke and Michael were already ahead of him up the street.

"Wait up, guys," he said.

Luke and Michael stopped and waited for him to catch up. Johnny ran up and walked in between the other two boys.

"I think we ran a thousand miles today," panted Johnny.

"Coach Krowley thinks we need to be in better shape for the next game," explained Luke.

"Milson General Store's team is small, but they are super fast," noted Michael.

"Yeah, but four days in a row of running is wearing me out!" complained Johnny.

"Are you ready for the vocabulary test tomorrow?" asked Michael.

"I suppose," answered Luke. "I hate vocab tests!"

A loud scraping noise behind them made the boys stop and turn around. Erik had just slid his board along the edge of a small brick wall that they had just passed. When he came to the edge of the wall he jumped down to the sidewalk and did a kickflip before he stopped.

"Hey Erik," said Johnny.

Erik nodded his head to say hello. He reached over and took Johnny's helmet and pads and put them on his skateboard. Then he took Michael's and Luke's gear and balanced them on top of Johnny's. Erik wheeled his skateboard and the pile of football gear down the street as they continued their walk home.

The four boys had walked almost a block when they heard the familiar sound of the ice cream truck coming up the street. The white truck, almost the shape of a large box, was lined with storage compartments with small doors. A large plastic ice cream cone rotated on the middle of the roof, and music blared at an obnoxious level from speakers at each of the four corners. The noise seemed to travel for miles.

Luke reached into his sock and pulled out some money. He waved at the truck, hoping to get the driver's attention.

"My treat today," said Luke. "I've got some money from mowing the lawn."

The sliding door on the side of the truck flew open and Raz looked down at the boys and gave them a sneer.

"What do you want," he snapped. "I don't have all day."

Erik was looking at the pictures on the side of the truck, trying to decide whether to have a dogface, a bomb pop, or a popsicle with bubble gum.

"C'mon. C'mon," urged Raz.

"How about four dogfaces, please," Luke said quickly.

Raz rolled his eyes at Pete and the two of them started making the cones.

"Can't you kids order anything else? I hate making these dogfaces!" whined Raz.

"Just a few more days and we'll be out of here," said Pete.

The boys got their dogface cones and started walking down the street. The big truck started blaring the music again and drove away.

"Those guys are really weird!" exclaimed Michael. "I've heard they live in the old Hanley Mansion on Manor Street."

"That old place? No one has lived there for years," said Johnny.

"My dad said they rented it for the summer. It is kinda creepy," added Michael.

The boys continued to walk and eat their cones for a block before Erik spoke up.

"Officer Bill is coming to school tomorrow," he said.

"I heard that too," said Luke.

Officer Bill lived in their neighborhood and the boys knew him well. Officer Bill was one of the best baseball players to ever play for Mapleville High School. He often played catch with the boys.

"I heard we are going to have a special assembly in the morning," added Luke.

"Maybe we will miss our vocab test!" Johnny said hopefully.

"Yeah right! I heard it was going to rain gumballs, too!" chuckled Michael.

Johnny looked up in the air and put out his hand as if testing for rain.

"You never know!" he laughed.

CHAPTER ELEVEN

"Anonymous. The donor to the school wished to remain anonymous," Mrs. G said as she read the last vocabulary word. "As soon as you have finished with your papers you can put them in the basket on my desk."

The bell rang just as the last student finished the test. Mr. Ackerman, the principal, announced on the intercom that the special assembly was about to begin. Mrs. G gathered all the students and they walked to the gymnasium along with the rest of the school.

The gym was full of students sitting on the wood floor. The teachers sat in chairs along the side wall while the kids stayed in groups depending on their grade. Mrs. G.'s class was in the back and the boys leaned against the back wall.

Mr. Ackerman tapped the microphone to make sure it was on and introduced Officer Bill.

Officer Bill, dressed in his blue Mapleville police uniform, walked up to the microphone.

"Good morning, students," he started. "I want to talk with you today regarding a serious issue here in Mapleville."

Many of the students turned to each other and began to whisper.

"As some of you may know, there are a number of pets missing in our community," Officer Bill continued. "We at the Mapleville police department believe that something illegal is going on."

"I knew he was going to say that!" whispered Johnny to the other boys.

"We would like all of you to watch your pets carefully and keep them on a leash," Officer Bill continued.

Mary Beth McDermott raised her hand and he called on her.

"What about cats?" asked Mary Beth. "They are difficult to put on a leash."

"Thanks for mentioning that, Mary Beth. I would recommend that you keep your cats inside and watch them carefully if you let them outside," replied Officer Bill.

A little boy in the front row raised his hand and stood up.

"Are you sure that the pets aren't being eaten by lions or tigers?" he said.

A huge roar of laughter came from the children in the gym. The little boy sat quickly and ducked his head.

"That's a very good question," noted Officer Bill.

Officer Bill raised both hands for quiet and the children slowly quieted down. Hoping to make the little boy feel better, he repeated it.

"That's a very good question," he said. "There are animals out there that could do something like this. It's possible a band of coyotes could be attacking the pets. We are looking into all the options."

"Cool, I say we go coyote hunting!" said Michael to Johnny and Luke.

Mrs. G heard Michael, put one finger to her mouth, and opened her eyes wider than normal.

"There is a reward being offered by many of the pets' owners for their return," Officer Bill continued. "Hopefully, we can figure this out and return the pets to their homes."

Principal Ackerman dismissed the assembly and the students walked back to class. The boys stopped outside Mrs. G's classroom.

"I think we should look for the pets. Let's have a stakeout tonight after practice," said Luke. "Bring some binoculars and walkie talkies. Wear dark clothes too."

"How about we eat dinner after practice, then have a stakeout," pleaded Michael.

"All he thinks about is food!" chuckled Johnny. "Ok, meet at the fort after dinner."

CHAPTER TWELVE

As soon as practice ended the boys gathered up their equipment and headed home. Erik showed up and loaded the shoulder pads and helmets on his skateboard.

"What are we going to stake out?" asked Johnny.

"I don't know. I thought we could look for suspicious activity or something," replied Luke.

"Can I help?" asked Erik.

"I don't see why not," said Michael.

Erik stopped and scratched his head. The other boys walked a couple steps more and then turned around.

"What's a stakeout?" asked Erik.

The other boys laughed a little and began to walk again. Erik hurried with the skateboard full of equipment and caught up.

"It's when you hide and wait for something to happen. Police do it to try and catch criminals," answered Johnny.

"James Bond does it all the time," said Michael.

The boys made pretend guns with their fingers and started shooting each other while humming the James

Bond theme song. Michael jumped and rolled on the grass as he aimed at Luke.

"Let's hurry up and eat so we can find the pets," said Johnny. "Meet at the fort."

The boys hurried home, ate, and changed their clothes. Johnny, Luke, and Erik, dressed in black shorts and dark shirts, waited at the fort. Johnny was carrying a backpack with binoculars and walkie talkies. Erik was carrying his skateboard and wearing his black helmet.

Michael rode up on his bike and stopped at the bottom of the fort.

"Man, it's hot out!" exclaimed Michael.

"It's because you're wearing a turtleneck!" cried out Johnny.

"It's the only black shirt I could find," replied Michael.

"Can you carry these?" added Michael.

"What is it?" asked Johnny.

"A big bag of chocolate chip cookies!" answered Michael. "I gotta feeling that we might get hungry on this stakeout stuff."

Johnny put them in his backpack and handed out the walkie talkies.

"We need some code names for tonight," stated Johnny. "How about stuff from James Bond?"

Luke decided he would be "Q," for a character in the movies, Johnny wanted to be James Bond, and Michael decided he would be "M," James Bond's boss.

"Erik can be The Skateboard King," said Luke. "It's not from James Bond but it's a good name."

"If we see something suspicious we can say something like Code Red," said Michael.

The boys all agreed and started off on their bikes. Erik rode his skateboard, holding on to the back of Luke's bike to keep up.

"Where are we going to set up our stakeout?" asked Michael. "Let's not go too far. I'm sweating."

"How about Wynn's hill?" asked Luke.

"Good idea, Luke. We can see a huge area from the top of the hill," said Johnny.

Wynn's Hill was a large sledding hill next to Mr. Wynn's house. In the winter the whole neighborhood would sled all day and Mr. Wynn would provide hot chocolate to the kids. The hill was surrounded by streets on three sides, and from the top you could see for blocks.

The boys decided to go to the top of the hill and spread out around the top to get the best view of the streets.

"How about I watch Ridge Street? Luke, you watch Hill Street, and Michael, you can watch Oak Street," suggested Johnny.

"Erik, why don't you ride your skateboard around and we'll keep in contact with the walkie talkies," said Luke.

The boys hid their bikes in the bushes and ran up the hill to take their positions.

CHAPTER THIRTEEN

"**M**, this is Q. Do you read me?" asked Luke into his walkie talkie.

"I read you, Q. Loud and clear," answered Michael.

"See anything yet?" asked Luke.

"Negative," said Michael.

The boys were about fifty yards apart, spread out over the top portion of Wynn's hill. The sun had set and it was beginning to get dark. Each of them was spread out on the ground, scouting the area with their binoculars.

"Johnny, I mean James Bond, do you read me?" asked Luke.

"I read you, nothing to report on Ridge Street," replied Johnny. "How does it look on Hill Street?"

"I can see Erik riding around, but nothing suspicious," said Luke.

For over an hour, the boys had nothing to report but the occasional car. Michael even reported on the nut gathering of a squirrel on Oak Street.

"Q here. We have a large truck approaching on Hill Street and turning on Oak Street," stated Luke.

"Hey, I can see a dog wandering around on Oak Street," said Michael.

"I can see a dog down on Ridge Street too," stated Johnny. "And there is a man walking toward it."

"Code Red to the Skateboard King! Code Red to the Skateboard King!" said Luke loudly into his walkie talkie. "You need to go to Ridge Street and check out the man following a dog!"

Michael and Luke both got up and ran to Johnny's side of the hill. The three boys watched the man following the dog through their binoculars. Erik was racing down the street on his skateboard, trying to get to the dog before the man did.

"We better get down there," Johnny said. "We can't let Erik face that man alone."

They ran down the hill as fast as their legs could run. The four boys reached the dog before the man was even close. Erik reached over and started to pet the dog.

"You can't steal this dog, Mister!" shouted Erik. "Don't come any closer!"

The man paused for a moment. It was difficult for the boys to see his face in the darkness. He resumed walking toward the boys until he finally came into view.

"Oh hi, Principal Ackerman," said Michael quickly. "We thought . . . "

"You thought I was stealing this dog," interrupted Principal Ackerman. "No, this is CoCo, my cocker spaniel. She got out and likes to run away."

"We're sorry. We were just on a stakeout looking for clues about the missing pets," said Luke.

"Don't be sorry. I don't mind," said Principal Ackerman. "If everyone keeps alert in the neighborhood, we will figure out what's happening."

"Thanks and good night," said Johnny.

Principal Ackerman picked up CoCo and walked back up the street towards his house.

"Good night boys and good work," he replied.

Johnny, Luke, and Michael picked up their hidden bikes and began to ride home. Erik was riding alongside the boys on his skateboard as they made the turn onto Oak Street.

"Sadie! Sadie!" came a voice from down the street.

"Sadie, come here girl!" said a little girl.

The boys rode down the block where a little girl was holding her father's hand.

"Have you seen my dog?" she asked. "We can't find her anywhere."

Johnny shook his head and the four boys tried to look for Sadie with no success. After the long search they all headed home, feeling awful.

"We did the code red on the wrong street," said Luke. "And now we have another missing dog."

"Michael, would you like your bag of cookies?" asked Johnny.

"I feel so bad I'm not even hungry," said Michael sadly.

Unless they figured out what was happening, they boys knew that their terrible feelings would only get worse.

CHAPTER FOURTEEN

The sun was shining and it was another beautiful afternoon for football. The crowd was pretty big for a Saturday game. The Mapleville Tire Center team was on the sideline waiting for the game to start. Johnny was throwing the football with Joey Spinelli on the field and coach Krowley was talking with the other coaches. Michael and Luke were sitting on the bench fiddling with their helmets. Megan, Johnny's sister, walked up to the bench.

"Hi Michael, Hi Luke," she said. "Have you seen Johnny?"

"He's over there. Why?" asked Luke.

"Well . . . , " she hesitated. "We can't find Jackson or Duke. We've looked everywhere. I have to tell Johnny."

Megan walked over to Johnny and quietly told him that his two dogs were missing. Johnny began to rub his eyes. He was obviously holding back tears.

The whistle blew for the game against Milson's General Store to begin. The boys gathered in the huddle before the kickoff.

"You okay?" Michael asked Johnny.

"Yeah, my dogs are missing," answered Johnny.

"We heard," said Luke.

"Let's get this game over with so I can find them," said Johnny.

The kick went high into the air and Johnny waited for it to drop from the sky. The ball was spinning end over end when it hit Johnny square in the chest. The ball bounced out in front of him and he dove on it just before the Milson General Store team.

"Sorry, guys," Johnny said as he entered the huddle.

Michael called a pass play to the right and the team broke from the huddle. The team lined up with Luke in the backfield and Johnny wide right. Joey Spinelli hiked the ball and Michael rolled toward the right sideline. He threw the football in a tight spiral right to Johnny's outstretched hands. Johnny turned to run upfield before he actually caught the ball and it fell, incomplete.

On the next play from scrimmage, Michael tossed the ball to Johnny on a sweep to the left. Johnny had troubled handling the toss and almost fumbled the ball. By the time he tucked the football away, he was tackled for a loss.

Coach Krowley sensed something wrong and substituted Danny J for Johnny. He put his arm around Johnny to talk to him on the sideline.

"What's up? I've never seen you run before you have the ball. You almost fumbled twice," he said.

Johnny couldn't hold it in any longer and a tear streaked down his cheek.

"We can't find our dogs at home. They are missing like all the other pets in Mapleville," he said.

Coach Krowley leaned over and put his hands on Johnny's shoulders and looked him in the eyes.

"I'm sure you will find them, Johnny. If you need to go home now, I'll understand," Coach said.

Johnny stood up straight and shook his head from side to side.

"No Coach. I want to play. I don't want to let my team down," stated Johnny.

Coach Krowley smiled and helped Johnny put his helmet back on.

"Then get out there and get your head in the game!" he exclaimed.

Johnny ran out to play defense since the Mapleville Tire Center team had already punted. Milson's General Store was on their own twenty with first and ten to go.

"They like to go wide and use their speed," said Michael from the huddle.

Milson's General Store hiked the ball and ran an option to their right. When the quarterback was about to be tackled he pitched the ball to the running back. After some nice blocking, the play went for about twenty yards.

Surprisingly, Milson's General Store ran the same play again to the same side and gained another ten yards to midfield.

Michael called for the boys to huddle and looked over to the sideline. Coach Krowley gave him a signal for the defense.

"I think they will try to go to their left this time. Johnny, you watch for the option," he said. "Ryan, I want you to cheat over at safety so he can make a play."

Johnny nodded and headed out to his position at cornerback. Milson's General Store hiked the ball and started to their left just as Michael had predicted. Michael avoided the first blocker and focused on tackling the quarterback. Johnny saw the option coming and let the wide receiver go behind him for Ryan to cover. When the quarterback pitched the ball, he darted forward and tipped the ball into the air.

"Grab the ball!" yelled Coach Krowley from the sideline.

Johnny was moving so fast that he passed the ball as it hung in the air. He spun around and reached out for the ball. His left hand almost caught the ball but it popped up again and landed on his right shoulder. He turned and continued running downfield when the ball finally rolled off into his shoulder into his hands. Without missing a stride, Johnny easily ran into the end zone.

Milson's General Store only got two more first downs in the first half. Their option play was ineffective now that the boys had figured out how to defend against it. Mapleville Tire Center never seemed to tire and won the game easily 35 to 0.

After the game, Johnny, Michael, and Luke quickly hurried home and began the search for Jackson and Duke. The boys rode their bikes around the neighborhood until dark to no avail. Johnny's dogs were gone for sure.

CHAPTER FIFTEEN

Johnny woke up early the next morning and dressed quickly. No one else was up as he went outside to get his bike. Waiting at the end of the driveway on their bikes were Luke and Michael. Erik was sitting on his skateboard next to the other two boys.

"What are you guys doing here?" asked Johnny.

"We figured you would keep looking so we decided to help," answered Luke.

Johnny didn't know what to say. He extended his fist and touched his knuckles to Michael and Luke. Erik jumped up off his skateboard and made a knuckle too. He stopped his hand just before it touched and looked up at the other boys. Johnny nodded his head and the four of them finished the unofficial handshake of the fort.

"Knuckles," they said softly.

The boys looked for Jackson and Duke until lunch without any luck. Johnny's mom had figured that the boys were out searching and had lunch ready when they returned. She took everything to the fort and even had some warm cookies. The boys settled into the bean bags and dug into the food.

"We've looked everywhere!" gasped Johnny.

"I know," said Luke. "We searched the neighborhood, the woods, the park, even the city garbage dump. I don't where else we'd look."

"I think we are going about it all wrong," said Michael. "Looking around for them isn't working. We are assuming that someone is stealing them, right?"

"Yeah, but why would anyone want to do that?" Johnny asked.

"Maybe to sell them or something," said Luke. "You know if you think about it, all the animals that are missing seem to be kind of special in one way or another."

"Mrs. Dunbar's cat is one of those long haired Persian ones. Mrs. G has that toy poodle. And Johnny, Duke and Jackson are really good hunting dogs," added Michael.

"Yeah, you're right guys! Isn't Mary Beth's a Siamese show cat?" asked Johnny.

"But who? Who is stealing them?" asked Luke.

The boys couldn't think of anyone who would do such a thing. They couldn't even think of one person.

"Maybe we could try another stakeout," suggested Michael.

"We would have to be really lucky to catch them like that. It didn't work last time," said Johnny.

"We have to find a way to catch the thief while he is stealing the animals," said Luke.

"We need to set a trap that can take us to all the pets," said Johnny.

The boys tried to come up with a plan, but nothing seemed like it could work. They were all about to give up when Erik stood up.

"GPS," he said.

"What?" asked Luke.

"A GPS, like the one Dad has," added Erik.

"What's a GPS?" asked Michael.

"It's a global positioning system device," answered Luke. "It's used for locating things by using satellites out in space. You can pinpoint where you are within feet. I think they even have them in phones these days."

"How would we use one of those?" asked Johnny.

"What if we . . . ," Michael paused and began again. "What if we put a phone on my dog Lucy and let her get captured? She could lead us to the rest of the pets."

"I'm not sure that's a good idea," said Johnny. "Your dad will be mad if you let your yellow Lab get stolen."

"Well, we just won't let that happen," said Michael.

"I suppose, but where would we find one of those phones?" asked Luke.

"Spinelli's Hardware Store," answered Michael. "He sells all kinds of phones."

CHAPTER SIXTEEN

The boys rode down to the hardware store and quickly located Mr. Spinelli. He was an expert on all kinds of electronics and anything mechanical.

"We need a phone with a GPS," said Luke. "It needs to be pretty small."

Mr. Spinelli took the boys to the part of the store with all the phones and showed them all the ones that fit what they wanted. He showed them one that was as small as a credit card and the boys agreed that was the one that they would need.

"What do you want it for?" asked Mr. Spinelli.

"We really don't want to say," answered Michael. "We only need it for a day, though."

"Why don't you ask Joey?" replied Mr. Spinelli. "That's the kind of phone he has. I think he is in the back of the store playing on the computer."

The four boys ran to the back of the store and told Joey of their plan. Joey wanted to help and showed them on his computer how he could track the exact location of his phone.

"See, the phone shows up at the hardware store where we are," said Joey. "I think if you guys tape it to Lucy's collar we can find her wherever she goes."

The boys finished with their plan and took Joey's miniature phone. They rode their bikes and skateboard to Michael's house and prepared Lucy for her mission.

"Lucy loves to run, so as soon as I let her out of the house we can go back to the hardware store," said Michael.

"How will we know that someone has her?" asked Luke.

"The GPS signal will stop moving!" said Michael.

Michael finished taping the phone to Lucy's collar and walked her out to the street.

"Find Jackson and Duke, Lucy," said Michael as he let her go.

Lucy took off down the street like a lightning bolt; she was gone within a few seconds.

By the time they had returned to the hardware store, Joey was already tracking Lucy's position.

"Wow!" he exclaimed. "Lucy's already been to Wynn's hill, the baseball field and the skateboard park."

The boys watched Lucy's path around Mapleville in amazement. For over two hours she ran from neighborhood to neighborhood.

"Does she ever stop?" asked Joey.

"When she comes home," laughed Michael.

"Wait a minute!" Johnny exclaimed, looking at the computer screen. "The signal has stopped!"

Joey punched some keys on the computer and zoomed in on the map.

"Lucy is all the way down on the end of Manor Street," noted Joey.

Johnny, Luke, and Michael ran out of the hardware store and jumped onto their bikes. Erik was close behind, trying to keep up.

"Wait up!" yelled Erik.

"You better stay here," said Luke. "It might be dangerous."

CHAPTER SEVENTEEN

The three boys pedaled almost a mile to Manor Street. When they got closer, they slowed as they reached the end of the street.

"It's the old Hanley place!" said Johnny.

"That's where I heard Pete and Raz live. Remember?" said Michael.

The old Hanley house at the end of Manor Street was surrounded by woods on three sides. It appeared to have at least two stories and an attic on top of that. The shingles were mostly gone and those remaining were hanging by a corner or completely upside down. The driveway circled around to the back of the house and no car was visible from the front.

"Let's sneak in through the woods over here," suggested Luke.

The boys ditched their bikes in some trees in the vacant lots next to the house and cautiously made it to the edge of the woods nearest the house.

"We need to cross over to the house," said Johnny. "I'll go first. I'll wave you over when I know the coast is clear."

Johnny stood behind a tree and peeked around it. He took a deep breath and raced over to the house. He stopped by a large window and peered inside. Since he didn't see anything, he motioned for Luke and Michael to follow.

"See anything inside?" whispered Luke as he tucked in behind Johnny.

"Nope, I've looked in both windows on this side of the house. Both rooms are empty," replied Johnny.

"Maybe we should try out back," suggested Michael.

Michael took the lead and crawled along the side of the house behind some bushes. There were plenty of places to hide along the house since most of it was covered with old vines and surrounded with overgrown shrubs. When he arrived at the corner of the house, he pushed some branches out of the way and poked his head through.

"There's the ice cream truck," he said.

Johnny and Luke climbed into the shrub at the corner so they could also see the back of the house and the truck.

The rear of the truck was facing the back porch. On either side of the porch was a trellis full of vines that reached to the second story.

"I'm gonna go look in the back door," whispered Luke.

Luke started to step out of the shrub when Johnny grabbed him by the back of the shirt and tugged him backward.

"There is someone coming," exclaimed Johnny.

The screen door swung noisily open on its hinges and Raz walked out onto the porch and hopped down to the ground, skipping the stairs. He walked to the back of the ice cream truck and leaned over to open a large compartment with the twist of a handle. He pulled a rope out of his back pocket and reached into the compartments with both hands. When he stood up he yanked a large yellow dog to the ground.

"It's Lucy!" Michael said, a little too loudly.

Johnny reached over and put his hand on Michael's mouth before he could say anything else.

Raz looked over in the direction of the shrubs, thinking he had heard something. He began to take a step toward the boys when the screen door opened again.

"C'mon. Hurry up!" yelled Pete. "Do I have to do everything around here?"

"I just thought," began Raz.

"Don't think," yelled Pete again. "You might hurt your brain!"

Pete started laughing and, luckily for the boys, Raz forgot the noise he'd heard from Michael's outburst.

"Now hurry up and get that dog in a cage," continued Pete. "Then we can finally load them up and get out of this town."

"I bet we can sell this one for a few hundred dollars," stated Raz as he walked onto the porch.

"Let's hurry so we can leave before dark," said Pete.

Pete opened the creaky door and followed Raz and the newly stolen Lucy into the house.

Johnny, Luke, and Michael settled onto the ground in the middle of the large shrub.

"Do you think we should go get some help?" asked Luke.

"We don't have time," answered Michael. "We have to get inside and let our pets free before it's too late."

"There's no way we can sneak in the back with that creaky door," noted Luke.

"Let's check out the other side of the house," said Johnny.

"What do we do then?" asked Luke. "What's the plan?"

Michael started crawling again and then turned his head toward Luke.

"James Bond doesn't always have a plan," he said.

CHAPTER EIGHTEEN

The boys crawled carefully around to the other side of the house. The overgrown shrubs and weeds provided all the cover they needed to stay hidden.

"There are some doors to the basement on this side of the house," said Johnny.

He flipped up the unlocked hinge on the double doors and the boys quietly lifted them open. Johnny started down the stairs and paused when he reached the bottom, trying to let his eyes adjust to the darkness. Luke and Michael followed closely behind and stopped as well.

The basement room they were in was damp and musty, and the floor was all concrete. Once their eyes had adjusted, the boys could see that the room was empty.

"There is a door on the other side of the room," Johnny said.

The boys made their way to the door. Johnny put his ear to the door and listened for a few seconds.

"Did you hear that?" asked Johnny.

"It sounds like whimpering," said Luke.

Johnny slowly opened the door, hoping not to make any noise. When the door was about half open, the three boys slid inside. A chorus of yelping and barking began almost immediately. Thirty or forty cages with all kinds of cats and dogs were lined up around the outside of the room. Some were even stacked on top of each other and on the steps leading upstairs.

"Duke, Jackson!" Johnny said as he ran to a cage to his right.

Michael ran over to the cage that Lucy was in and opened the door.

"Let's get all the animals out of the cages and get them out through the basement door," said Luke.

"NOT SO FAST!" yelled Raz from the bottom of the steps.

Pete was standing next to him with a large baseball bat in his hands.

"I wouldn't touch any of those cages," snarled Pete.

The three boys froze and then stood up. Luke put his hands in the air and then quickly put them down.

"Upstairs!" yelled Raz. "Now!"

Johnny, Michael, and Luke reluctantly started up the stairs behind Raz. Pete walked closely behind, tapping his hand with the bat.

"What should we do with them?" asked Raz.

"We'll tie them up in one of the rooms upstairs and then finish loading the cages onto the truck," answered Pete. "We'll be long gone before anyone finds them."

Raz marched the boys up the long winding flight of the stairs to the second floor of the once majestic old house. The banister along the stairs must have been over fifty feet long and a large chandelier hung down from the ceiling. Raz pushed them along, guided them into a room at the back of the house, and began to tie them to some old wooden chairs.

"What are you doing this for?" asked Luke.

"What a stupid question," snapped Raz.

"Money," added Pete as he entered the room. "We'll sell all those animals for thousands and thousands of dollars."

"It beats making dogface ice creams for you punks!" yelled Raz.

"We called the police already," threatened Michael. "They will be here any minute."

"Nice try, punk," said Raz. "We would have heard sirens by now."

"And don't bother yelling because no one can hear you!" added Pete. "That's why we chose this house. It's surrounded by woods at the end of a street."

Johnny wiggled and pulled violently against the ropes that tied him to the chair. Pete and Raz just laughed at him and started to walk out of the room.

"Let's load up those cages and get out of here," instructed Pete.

Pete and Raz walked into the hallway and down the stairs.

CHAPTER NINETEEN

"What are we gonna do now?" asked Michael. "My hands are tied so tight I can't move," noted Johnny.

Michael tried to turn his chair around backwards so his hands were toward Johnny's hands. He tried to untie Johnny but couldn't grip the rope to loosen it.

"Help! Help!" yelled Luke.

"It's no use Luke, Raz is right. We are too far for anyone to hear," stated Johnny.

"I can't believe this!" exclaimed Michael. "We have to get out of here or those guys are going to drive away with our dogs!"

"I think I can stand up a little," said Johnny.

"That won't do any good, Johnny. You can't jump out the second story window and you certainly can't go down all those stairs," explained Michael.

After shifting the chairs around trying to untie the ropes, the boys wound up almost facing each other in a small circle.

"I'm really sorry, guys," said Luke "I don't know what I would do if I lost my . . . . . "

He stopped as a skateboard rolled in between the three boys. Johnny, Luke, and Michael turned and looked in the direction of the window.

"Where did that come from?" asked Michael.

Two small hands grabbed at the window sill and up popped Erik's head.

"ME! Silly!" exclaimed Erik.

"I thought we told you to stay at the hardware store," scolded Luke.

"I thought you guys might need some help!" Erik said.

"Well I'm glad you didn't listen," said Johnny. "See if you can untie these ropes."

Erik reached down and started undoing the knots binding Luke's hands. It didn't take him long before all three boys were free.

"How did you get up here?" asked Johnny.

"I climbed up those vines next to the window," answered Erik.

"And you brought your skateboard?" questioned Luke.

"Well, I wasn't going to leave it down there!" answered Erik.

The boys gathered in a small huddle near the window.

"We have to get out of here and get help," said Johnny.

"I could climb back down and find Officer Bill," said Erik.

Erik stuck his foot out the window to climb out. Michael grabbed Erik from behind and pulled him back in the room.

"Get down!" exclaimed Michael. "Here comes Pete."

The boys heard the screen door slam and Pete walked toward the ice cream truck; he was carrying a cage with a small dog inside. After he put the cage in the truck he headed back inside.

"I don't think we can get down that way. They will be sure to see us," noted Michael.

"We'll have to go down the stairs," said Luke.

Johnny nodded and headed for the door. He peered around the edge of the door and walked out into the hall. Luke followed right behind and crouched behind the railing at the top of the stairs. Johnny carefully stepped onto the top stair and the wooden stair creaked slightly. Raz had just turned the corner below them and looked up to see the boys.

"Pete!" he yelled. "Those knuckleheads got loose!"

Raz started running up the long winding stairway two or three steps at a time. Michael saw him coming and climbed up on the railing. He dove out into mid-air and grabbed the chandelier. His body swung forward and then back and forward again. Raz was almost to Johnny and Luke when Michael launched into the air. Johnny kicked as hard as he could while Luke swung as hard as he could with his fist. Michael landed on the top of Raz at the same time that Johnny and Luke connected. Raz flew backward down the stairs, head over heels.

"I got you!" said Johnny as he grabbed Michael and prevented him from the same fall as Raz.

Raz was sprawled out at the bottom of the steps, moaning. Pete was watching from below and started up the stairs much more slowly and carefully than Raz had done. Johnny, Luke, and Michael backed up slightly, knowing they would not be as lucky taking care of Pete as they had with Raz.

"WATCH OUT!" yelled Erik as he rolled down the hallway on his skateboard.

Erik pushed a few times and quickly gained some speed. He crouched down slightly and pressed his feet into the board, then jumped upward, lifting himself and the board into the air. The bottom of his board made contact with the wooden banister and Erik was on top of it, balanced in the middle. He rode the board down the banister with his hands outstretched, keeping him balanced.

"Board slide!" announced Luke.

Erik crouched again as he came near the bottom. Pete started backing up but couldn't move fast enough for the fast approaching skateboarder. Erik popped the board up with his feet and slammed the bottom of it into Pete's nose.

"Yeah!" yelled the boys in unison.

Pete fell backwards over Raz, completely knocked out. Erik landed miraculously on his board and thumped down the rest of the stairs. He hopped off his board and pumped his fist in the air.

"Skateboard King!" yelled Johnny.

Raz moaned again and tried to get to his feet.

"I'm gonna get you punks!" he yelled.

Erik lifted his board with two hands and crashed it down on Raz's head. The board broke in two pieces and Raz crumpled back to the ground.

All the excitement escaped from Erik's face as held a half of a skateboard in each hand.

"My board!" he groaned. "Not my board!"

CHAPTER TWENTY

Principal Ackerman stood in front of the microphone waiting for the children to quiet down. The Mayor of Mapleville and Officer Bill were seated next to the podium on the left. Many of the residents of Mapleville were also in attendance. The entire gym of Holy Spirit School was bustling with excitement.

"I would like you all to welcome the mayor to our school," announced Principal Ackerman.

Michael leaned over to Luke and whispered, "I've got a stomach ache."

"I'm not surprised," Luke whispered back. "You almost ate the entire batch of brownies from Mrs. Dunbar."

Everyone clapped loudly for the Mayor of Mapleville and quickly quieted down as he walked to the podium.

"I am here today with Officer Bill to recognize four young men for their bravery," said the mayor. "Without them, many of our beloved pets would have been lost forever."

The mayor told the story of the boys catching the criminals and returning the stolen pets to their rightful owners.

"Their courage is an example to all. On behalf of the citizens of Mapleville we thank you," he continued. "If you boys would please stand, we would like to present each of you with a medal for courage and bravery."

Johnny, Luke, Michael, and Erik rose and stood to the right of the podium. Officer Bill placed a medal around each of their necks and shook their hands. When he was finished, the gym erupted in applause. After a short while, the mayor raised his hands for quiet and began to speak again.

"I want you all to know that the reward posted by the owners of the missing pets has been donated to the local animal shelter by request of the boys," he said. "However, we have learned that something was broken during the apprehension of the criminals."

The mayor reached down behind the podium and picked up a brand new skateboard.

"All the students of Holy Spirit have chipped in to buy Erik a new skateboard," he said as he handed it to Erik.

Everyone in the gym was standing and clapping. Some of the kids in Erik's class started chanting, "Skateboard King! Skateboard King!" Eventually everyone joined in.

"Way to go, guys," said Johnny as he made a fist. Michael, Luke, and Erik made fists too and they touched them together.

"Knuckles," the boys yelled.

It was going to be a very good year.

The Cruise Caper

To Mo and Meggie for your encouragement

CHAPTER ONE

The snow was falling so heavily outside that the boys couldn't see their fort from inside the house. Normally the boys would be in the fort no matter the temperature. They would just use the blankets that they kept in there. Today, however, was quite different because it wasn't only cold, but very windy too.

"Maybe we can get your dad and grandpa to put a heater in the fort," said Michael. "Then we could go out there all the time."

Johnny nodded as he turned on the video game console. Luke and Michael were already sitting in their bean bags with game controllers in their hands.

"Bond or NBA?" asked Johnny.

"BOND!" Luke and Michael screamed together.

Although watching James Bond movies in the fort was their favorite thing to do, playing a James bond video game wasn't far behind. As the theme song started to play, the three boys pointed their fingers and pretended to shoot each other.

When the music ended, the boys settled into their beanbags and began to play the game.

"Got him!" said Luke. "Look out behind you, Johnny."

"I see him," replied Johnny.

"I'll get him before he catches up to you," said Michael. The boys talked and played the multiplayer game for almost an hour. Johnny's dad came into the room and sat down on the couch behind them.

"Hey boys," he said. "How's it going?"

"Great, Dad," answered Johnny. "We've been getting rid of the bad guys."

"Nice shot, Michael!" noted Johnny's dad. "You boys should wrap it up soon because you have a basketball game tonight."

"In a minute, Dad," replied Johnny.

"I can't wait for tonight!" added Luke. "I'm sure glad I decided to play basketball this year."

"Me too! I'm sure glad we have someone else to handle the ball," said Johnny.

"It should be a tough game tonight. They have Doug Wright on their team," said Johnny's dad.

"He's awesome!" added Michael.

"Yeah, they beat the last team they played by twenty-six points," said Luke. "and Doug had most of their points!"

Hey Dad, do you want to play James Bond with us?" asked Johnny.

"Hmmm, well I do need to pack since we leave for spring break in a couple of days," said Johnny's dad, "but I guess a couple of minutes wouldn't hurt."

Johnny plugged in another controller and handed it to his dad, who slid down into a beanbag.

"Look out behind you, Luke," said Michael.

"Wow," exclaimed Michael. "That was a great shot!"

"Thank you very much, Michael," said Johnny's dad.

The three boys and Johnny's dad all touched their knuckles together. Touching their knuckles together was the unofficial handshake of the fort.

A few minutes later, Michael and Luke got up in order to go home and get ready for the basketball game. Johnny followed them to the steps.

"Hey Dad, you should wrap it up soon," Johnny said jokingly.

Johnny's dad, staring at the screen, mumbled, "In a minute."

The three boys laughed as they climbed upstairs.

"He's gonna be playing a lot longer than that!" said Michael.

As the boys came upstairs, Johnny's mom greeted them with a freshly baked plate of cookies.

"Where's your dad, Johnny?" she asked. "I sent him down to get you guys twenty minutes ago."

"He said he'd be up in a minute," said Johnny as he took a bite of his cookie.

"Oh my, not again," said Johnny's mom. "The last time he did this he played for two hours! Anyway, you boys get ready for basketball and I'll go get Johnny's dad."

CHAPTER TWO

The boys carried their basketball shoes as they ran to the school through the howling winds. The snow was piled high from a winter of snowstorms and icicles hung from the edges of the building. As they opened the door, a gust of cold air almost pushed them inside.

"It's freezing out there," said Luke. "I can't wait to go on spring break with you guys!"

"The cruise ship is huge!" exclaimed Johnny.

"Hey guys, we have other things to worry about," stated Michael as he waved at Doug Wright.

"How are we gonna stop him?" whispered Luke.

"Coach Donaker will have a plan. He always does," said Johnny. "We beat Sacred Heart for the championship last year. We can beat these guys."

"You guys never played Doug last year though," said Luke shaking his head.

The gym was pretty full with fans. Even some of the girls in their class had come to watch.

"Hey Luke, there is Mary Beth McDermott sitting next to Suzie!" said Johnny as he chuckled behind his hand.

"Aw man, she tried to kiss me again the other day," complained Luke. "Why me? I don't get it!"

"Maybe she likes blond boys?" said Michael.

"You guys are blond," Luke stated.

Johnny and Michael just shrugged their shoulders and ran out onto the court to warm up with the rest of the Holy Spirit Jaguar team.

On the other side of the court, the team from Holy Angels was warming up as well. Doug Wright was shooting from all over the court, barely missing any shots.

"Boys, over here," said Coach Donaker, waving the boys to the side.

The whole team ran over toward Coach and made a small circle around him.

"I know you are all worried about the other team tonight," Coach said.

"No, we are just worried about Doug Wright!" exclaimed Billy Thomas, the tallest player on the Jaguars.

"Thank you, Billy. That is exactly my point. We are not just playing Doug Wright tonight. We are playing the Holy Angels team," said Coach Donaker.

"But he's really good!" Luke said quickly.

"He sure is, Luke. But if you boys play well as a team, you can beat anyone!" Coach said. "Don't worry at all. We'll figure out their weakness. Now go out there and play hard!"

All the boys placed their hands in the middle of the circle and yelled "Jaguars!" in unison.

CHAPTER THREE

Billy Thomas won the jump ball and pushed it toward Michael. Michael gave the ball to Johnny, who was playing point guard. Johnny looked up court toward Luke and Danny J and decided to dribble the ball down the court himself.

Coach Donaker had worked very hard all season on new offensive plays. In order to make them easy to remember, he named them after college basketball teams.

"UCLA," Coach yelled to Johnny.

Johnny nodded, quickly moved the ball to his right, and fired a pass to Michael. Michael ran toward the ball and almost as fast as he caught it he passed it to Billy, who was moving into the lane toward the basket. Billy turned to shoot a layup when out of nowhere Doug Wright stuffed his shot back and stole the ball. He started up the court and drove past Danny J and made an easy two-point layup.

"This is gonna be a long night," said Luke as he passed in the ball to Johnny.

"Keep your heads up guys!" encouraged Michael.

Coach Donaker was walking up the sideline scratching his head. "Duke!" he yelled.

This time Johnny faked to his right and passed the ball to Luke as he moved around Danny J, who set a pick for him. Luke moved nearer the lane and took a quick shot for an easy two points.

"Way to go, Luke!" yelled Johnny as he touched his knuckle to his Luke's while running back on defense.

Doug Wright dribbled the ball down the court and held two fingers in the air. He dribbled with his right hand and switched the ball to his left. As soon as Danny J moved a little toward the ball, Doug switched the dribble back to his right hand and drove right past Danny. No one was in position to stop Doug and he tossed in another easy layup.

The rest of the first half included more of the same kinds of moves from Doug Wright. Doug would move the ball left and right until he found an opening and then drive to the basket. Occasionally he would pass to someone else, but mostly he shot the ball himself. It was a hard fought game with lots of jump balls and blocked shots.

At halftime, the Holy Spirit Jaguars were losing by only five points, 20 to 15. Michael had kept the game close by shooting two three-pointers. He'd been working hard on his shooting and his improved form was paying off.

"Get a drink and rest a little," Coach Donaker said, pointing directly at Danny J, whose face was bright red from covering Doug Wright.

"Not bad boys, but we won't win if we don't stop them from scoring," said Coach Donaker. "Johnny, let's run the Tarheel play and get a quick two points to start the half."

It was the Jaguars' turn to take out the ball after the last jump ball, and Johnny quickly dribbled the ball to the three-point line in the middle of the court. Danny J and Billy quickly moved up and set a double pick for Johnny. Johnny moved to his right and with two quick steps he was by his defender and shot a ten footer that swished the net.

"Nice move, Johnny!" Coach Donaker screamed.

The Holy Angels team quickly responded by moving the ball down the court and passing the ball to Doug Wright again. Doug dribbled right and left and then moved to his right, leaving Danny J behind him again. Doug easily slashed toward the basket for another layup.

With only one minute and twelve seconds left to go, the Holy Spirit Jaguars still trailed by four points and couldn't trim the Holy Angels' lead any more than that. Every time the Jaguars would score, Doug Wright would answer with a basket of his own. The score was 41 to 37 and Doug had twenty-five of the Holy Angels' points.

"Time out!" Coach Donaker yelled to the referee.

The boys ran to the bench and grabbed their water bottles as they sat down.

"I can't stop him!" exclaimed Danny J. "I'm exhausted, and he dribbles so well!"

Coach Donaker smiled at Danny J and took a deep breath.

"Don't worry, Danny. You've done a fine job. Every other team that has played Holy Angels has lost by twenty points," Coach said calmly. "I've been watching Doug very closely and I think I've figured out how to stop him. Johnny, since Danny is worn out, I want you to cover Doug Wright."

Johnny's eyes opened as wide as pancakes, but he didn't say anything.

"He always goes to his right when he drives for the basket," Coach said. "So when he dribbles to the left, make him think that you are going to cover him that way. When he moves his dribble back to his right, steal the ball down low to the ground. Luke and Michael, be ready to run a fast break for a layup."

Johnny nodded and ran out to the court as the buzzer sounded. Michael tapped his knuckles to Johnny's fist.

"He always goes to his right," restated Michael.

Johnny nodded again and crouched low in a defensive position.

The Holy Angels team took the ball out and again quickly put the ball into Doug Wright's hands. Doug held up his hand to signal the play. He moved the ball slowly up the court to use up some of the time on the clock. As he crossed over the half court line, Johnny moved up to defend him. Doug started dribbling right and left, preparing to drive to the basket. When Doug dribbled far to his left Johnny leaned in that direction and made Doug think he had him beat. Doug then moved to dribble with his right hand. Just as the ball was about to hit the ground, Johnny stuck out his hand with his palm up and deflected the ball. Luke saw the ball come loose and took off down the court. Johnny dove for the ball and passed it toward Luke during his dive.

"Nice steal, Johnny!" yelled Michael as Luke made a layup.

The crowd was on its feet, excited by the close game. The Holy Angels coach yelled for a time out and both teams returned to their benches.

"Good work, Johnny," said Coach Donaker. "It's a two-point game. We need the ball back and we need to score."

"Steal the ball again, Johnny!" exclaimed Billy.

"It's not going to be that easy. Doug is going to be ready for Johnny this time," said Coach as he grabbed his pen so he could diagram a play. "This time I want Luke to come and double team Doug when he tries to fake to his left. Luke, make sure you move close to his right and hold your hands up high. You and Johnny either need to steal the ball or not let him pass. With only thirty-five seconds left we have to act fast, so let's press them to start and maybe we can steal the ball."

The boys were looking at Coach Donaker's clipboard trying to figure out all the x's and o's when the buzzer sounded to start play again.

Doug quickly got the pass, broke the press easily, and moved into the frontcourt. He was dribbling the ball up at the top of the key when Johnny gave Luke a quick nod. Johnny moved up to defend Doug with his hands stretched out to his side. Doug, as usual, started dribbling left and right. When he finally made his move to the left to fake out Johnny, Luke quickly snuck over, preparing to get in Doug's way on the right. Johnny and Luke collapsed on Doug with their hands out-stretched and waving all over the place. Doug picked up his dribble and panicked, trying to find someone to pass to. The ball came loose and bounced in Michael's direction. Michael picked up the ball and started drib-bling as fast as he could down the court.

"Five, Four, Three!" screamed Coach Donaker.

At two seconds to go, Michael stopped short of the three-point line and decided to launch a shot. He looked down at his feet to make sure he was behind the line and let the ball fly. The ball arched way into the air and bounced hard on the back of the rim. When the ball came down again, it caught the front of the rim and hung there for a fraction of a second. The crowd became quiet and then erupted as the ball fell backward into the basket.

"Three! We win! We win!" screamed Luke and Johnny together.

Everyone was jumping up and down around Michael near the three-point line. When the Jaguars settled down, they shook the hands of the Holy Angels boys and congratulated them on a hard fought game.

Coach Donaker waved the boys over to the bench and huddled them together.

"That was an outstanding team effort, boys. Good players look good, but teams win basketball games," he said. "Have fun on spring break next week and play some basketball if you can."

The boys gathered up their shoes and gear and walked over to their families.

"Michael, game ending three-pointers are beginning to be your specialty," Johnny kidded him.

"Yeah, you are on a roll!" added Luke. "Last year's championship and now a game this year!"

"Well, like Coach said, it's a team game and your defense is what won it for us," replied Michael.

Just then Michael's dad walked up to the boys with a large grin on his face.

"Ice cream's on me," he said.

"Your dad always buys the ice cream," whispered Luke.

"He loves it so much he just looks for an excuse to go to the ice cream store," Michael whispered back.

"One more day of school until spring break and we won the basketball game and now ice cream. It can't get any better than this!" exclaimed Johnny as he made a fist toward the other boys.

"Knuckles!" they all yelled.

CHAPTER FOUR

The boys walked into class together and sat down at their desks. Mrs. Greenfield was writing on the chalkboard, preparing for the day.

"Good morning, boys," she said.

"Good morning, Mrs. G," the boys said almost in unison.

"I'm sure glad we got Mrs. G again," Luke whispered to Michael.

At the beginning of the year the boys had expected to have Mrs. Crabtree. She was known for being grumpy and not liking recess. Right before school started, though, Mrs. Crabtree decided to retire and the principal moved Mrs. Greenfield up a grade. That meant the boys would have her two years in a row.

"Yeah, a year without recess would be miserable," said Michael.

The bell rang and the rest of the students took their seats.

"I know that tomorrow is the first day of spring break, so I want you all to work hard this morning," said Mrs. Greenfield. "And then later today, we will have a special visitor come and talk to us."

"Who is it?" pleaded Suzie.

"Officer Bill from the police department is going to talk to us about what he does," Mrs. Greenfield said proudly.

"Cool!" said Johnny. "He lives right down the street from us."

The boys had known Officer Bill for as long as they could remember. He was one of the best baseball players to ever play for Mapleville high school. He once pitched a no-hitter and had a home run in the same game. When Officer Bill was not working, the boys would often play catch with him in the neighborhood.

"He has a really mean curveball!" exclaimed Luke.

"Well he isn't coming to our class to talk sports today," Mrs. G said, laughing. "He is going to talk to us about what a policeman does. Now, everyone stand up and let's say the Pledge of Allegiance."

School seemed to drag on forever, and the boys were anxious to end the day. Even gym class was boring, because Mr. Krowley had decided to teach badminton. The only thing that seemed to go quickly was lunch. Mrs. Franklin, the school cook, had prepared rotini twists and breadsticks. The boys would hollow out the breadsticks and stuff the rotini and sauce into the middle, making what they called "Rotini Breadsticks."

When they returned to class, Officer Bill was talking to Mrs. G and looking at pictures of her twins, Robert and Ryan. After everyone was seated at their desks, Mrs. G. stood up to address the class.

"I would like everyone to welcome Officer Bill to our class today; please give him your full attention."

Officer Bill walked to the front of the classroom and took off his hat. He was dressed in his blue police uniform with a Mapleville Police emblem on his chest.

"Hi kids. I am really excited to talk to you about police work today," said Officer Bill. "Oh yeah, before I start, congratulations to your basketball team on that big win last night!"

"I knew he would talk about sports," whispered Michael to Johnny.

Officer Bill began talking about the different laws and the reasons to obey them. He then talked about people who break the laws and how the police catch them. Everyone was very interested, especially when he showed them the handcuffs and other items that he had to carry with him.

"How do you know who breaks the laws?" asked Joey Spinelli.

"Well, sometimes we catch criminals in the act of breaking the law, but most of our work is done after a crime has already been committed," said Officer Bill.

Danny R raised his hand. "How do you know who committed the crime?"

"Well, we have to use evidence to lead us to the criminals," noted Officer Bill. "A police officer has to be very observant."

"What do you mean?" asked Johnny.

"Well, there are many things that an officer might use to solve a crime. We search for clues that tell us something about the person," explained Officer Bill. "It is very important to use the power of observation."

"What's a power of observation?" asked Mary Beth.

"That's a good question," he said. "The power of observation involves using your senses for information. For example, you might smell something or see something that might tell you who the criminal is."

Officer Bill could tell that the children were a little confused.

"How about an example," he said. "Let's just say that someone in this room stole an apple off of Mrs. Greenfield's desk while you all were out to lunch."

Officer Bill walked over to Mrs. G's desk and started to look around. He walked around to the back of the desk and pointed at the floor.

"What if I told you that there is a large muddy footprint over here," said Officer Bill.

"Billy Thomas stole it!" exclaimed Michael.

Everyone one in the class laughed because not only was Billy tall, but he also had big feet.

"I wouldn't say the footprint is that big," said Officer Bill. "I think we can just say that it didn't come from anyone small."

Just then, Officer Bill pulled a magnifying glass from his pocket. He put it in front of one of his eyes and looked down at the area where the apple might have been.

"I think I've found a brown hair on the desk," he said.

"That rules us out!" exclaimed Johnny, looking at Michael and Luke.

"Yes, I think I would agree," replied Officer Bill. "Ok, so what clues do we have? A larger foot and a brown hair, right?"

Officer Bill again put the magnifying glass in front of his eye and looked back down at the desk.

"Aha, another clue!" he said. "It seems to be a drop of something red."

Officer Bill took his finger and swiped it on the desk. He moved his finger in front of his nose and sniffed.

"Hmmm, seems to be," he said as his voice trailed off.

Then Officer Bill licked the end of his finger.

"Ewww!" screamed a few of the girls in the class.

"Spaghetti sauce!" he exclaimed.

Everyone turned in the direction of Joey Spinelli, or Joey Spaghetti as everyone called him. Joey was the biggest boy in the whole class, and he always had some of his lunch or dinner, usually spaghetti sauce, somewhere on his shirt.

"Hey, it wasn't me!" protested Joey.

Officer Bill walked over to Joey's desk and opened it. He reached down and pulled a large red apple out of the desk.

"I swear I didn't put it there!" Joey cried out.

"I know you didn't, Joey. I did, while you all were out at lunch," said Officer Bill. "I just used it as an example to show you all how to use clues and the power of observation."

Everyone in the class started laughing, including Joey. He was even happier when Officer Bill threw him the apple and told him he could eat it.

Officer Bill continued to talk about police work until the bell rang and school was over.

Everyone thanked Officer Bill and said goodbye to Mrs. G as they raced out the door. Spring break had begun.

CHAPTER FIVE

The flight on the airplane wasn't too long and the bus ride took about an hour. In the distance the boys could see the large cruise ship.

"Did you bring the basketball?" asked Michael.

"I told you they have them on the ship," replied Johnny.

"Wow, look at the size of the ship! It gets bigger and bigger the closer we get!" said Luke.

"My sister is going to be sad she didn't come along," Johnny said.

"She will have fun skiing with my family," answered Michael. "Besides I heard Kevin was going skiing at the same place with his family."

"I should have guessed," said Johnny.

Everyone got off the bus and went into the terminal next to the ship in order to check in and get their room cards. After a short wait, Johnny's parents and the boys walked down the gangplank onto the boat.

A group of crew members stood at the entrance.

"Welcome to the Regal Crown Cruise Line. I am Olaf Svensen, Captain of the Emerald of the Seas. We are very happy to have you aboard!" said the captain.

He leaned over a bit and held out his hand to the boys.

"And you are?" he asked.

"I'm Johnny and these are my best friends, Michael and Luke," replied Johnny.

"You young gentlemen are in for a wonderful week," the captain said. "If there is anything I can do for you, please find me, Captain Olaf, or any of my crew."

The captain turned back to greet more of the incoming guests, and other members of the crew introduced themselves as the boys moved into ship.

The entryway opened up into a very large atrium that was about three or four stories tall.

"This ship is huge!" exclaimed Luke. "Look at the stairway."

The stairwell was made mostly of glass and circled upward to the top of the atrium.

"I brought the walkie talkies," said Michael. "This ship is so big I think we are going to need them."

Michael handed one to Luke and one to Johnny.

"This is Bond, James Bond," said Johnny into the walkie talkie.

"What floor is our room on?" said Luke into his.

"Deck 9," said Johnny. "Our room is right next to my parents."

The boys walked down to the end of the atrium. A crew member was standing next to an ice cream machine, cleaning the area around it.

"How much is the ice cream?" asked Michael.

"It's free," the crew member replied. "All the food on the ship is free. Would you like some?"

"Are you kidding?" exclaimed Michael. "I'd love some!"

"This is gonna be awesome!" said Luke as he waited for his cone.

"We'll meet you at the room," Johnny said to his parents.

The boys started up the stairs with big smiles on their faces and ice cream in their hands.

CHAPTER SIX

Johnny slid his room card into the door and swung the door open. The room had three beds; two stood on the floor and one was flipped down from the wall.

"I get the bunk bed," said Michael.

"I don't think so," said Luke. "It's mine."

"Rock, paper, scissors," Johnny said.

After a few minutes of battle, Luke won with a rock to Johnny's scissors.

"Look at what's on the bed," said Johnny, pointing to a towel.

"Yeah, it's in the shape of an elephant!" said Luke. "That must have taken a while to make."

The boys were looking out the window at the water when a they heard a knock on the door.

"Come in," said Johnny.

The door opened and a short, dark-skinned man walked into the room. He wore a vest and a bow tie and had a large, toothy smile.

"Hello, young men. My name is Balde and I will be your cabin steward," he said. "Is this your first time on a cruise?"

"Yep," said Luke. "And I think I want to live here!"

"I know what you mean," he said. "It is a beautiful boat."

"Did you make the elephant?" asked Johnny. "It sure looks hard to make."

"It's not hard at all; let me show you," said Balde as he sat down on the edge of the bed. Michael and Luke ran into the bathroom to get their own towels. Balde twisted and shaped the towel into another elephant, showing the boys the method. After a while all three were twisting and folding, and soon they had all created elephants of their own.

"How long have you been working on the ship, Balde?" asked Luke.

"I have been working on ships for about four years," he said.

"Four years in a row?" asked Johnny.

"No, I work for six months and then get to go home to my family in India for two months," Balde said.

"That's a long time to be away from home," stated Johnny. "I wouldn't like it."

"It's not too bad. Besides, I get to meet a lot of nice people and I like my job," said Balde. "And I get to live on this beautiful boat."

"That is a good point," said Michael. "Luke, you should get a job here!'

Balde stood up and reached into the pocket of his vest.

"Here are some chocolates for you. I usually put them on your beds at night, but I think you young men could use a treat," said Balde as he handed them each a few pieces of chocolate. "I should go visit other cabins and meet some of the other guests."

"See you later," Johnny said as he stuffed a chocolate square into his mouth.

Just as Balde was about to leave, he stuck his head back into the room.

"Oh, and don't forget. There is a bon voyage party on the top decks right now. You don't want to miss it!" he said.

Michael turned to the other boys. "Let's go. Oh, and on the way we should stop on the atrium floor and get another ice cream."

CHAPTER SEVEN

The decks at the top of the boat were filled with people dancing and singing to the music of a band positioned near the center of the boat, just off the pool. Notable excitement arose when a loud blast of the boat horn signaled that the cruise ship was beginning to leave the harbor.

"You boys want a Beach Blast?" asked one of the crew members.

"What's in it?" Johnny asked.

"It's a frozen slushy with guava, mango, and strawberries. It even comes with a souvenir cup," said the crew member.

Johnny looked at his dad, who nodded yes.

"Here you go boys," said the crew member.

"Excellent!" said Luke.

"The boys walked over near the band and listened to their music. Johnny's dad had told them it was a reggae band from Jamaica. The boys were particularly interested in the drummer who was playing a drum made from the bottom side of a steel barrel. When the band stopped playing, the drummer waved them over.

"Hello, cruise boys, do you want to see my steel drum?" he said. "My name is Richard. Nice to meet you."

The boys introduced themselves and shook Richard's hand. Richard wore a flowery shirt and had lots of gold necklaces and gold rings on his fingers.

"How does it work?" asked Johnny.

"Each one of the dented looking areas represents a note," replied Richard. "Here, give it a try."

Luke took one of the drumsticks and started banging on the steel drum. Each of the boys took a turn and made some sounds. The cruise director of the ship grabbed one of the microphones and introduced himself to all the people on the top deck of the ship.

"Hey cruise boys, grab some tambourines and the cowbell over there," Richard said. "We can use some help on the next songs."

The cruise director put the microphone back and the band started to play again. Richard nodded at the boys and they played along with the music. Johnny's mom came running over with her camera and started taking pictures.

"This is embarrassing," said Johnny.

"She gonna show these all over Mapleville," whined Luke.

Everyone at the bon voyage party was having a great time dancing and singing to the music, already enjoying their cruise. It seemed that nothing could be more perfect than a vacation on the Emerald of the Seas.

CHAPTER EIGHT

Once the deck party started to slow down, the boys asked Johnny's parents if they could go explore the boat. They agreed and suggested they all meet for dinner in a couple hours.

"Let's take the elevator," suggested Luke. "It will be quicker."

The boys took the elevator down to Deck 2. It took quite a while to walk from one end of the boat to the other. There were signs all over the walls to help determine your location. They learned that the terms for front and back of a boat were forward and aft. The left side of the boat was port and the right was starboard. Most of Deck 2 was staterooms just like their room on Deck 9.

"Let's try another floor," suggested Michael.

The boys ran to the elevator and decided to push the button for Deck 12. The elevator had one wall made of glass and they could see the inside of the cruise ship as they rose quickly to the top level. The door opened into a very large, circular room filled with small tables around a large bar situated in the middle. The room was empty except for a bartender. Windows looking out over the sea surrounded the room. The boys walked over to the edge and looked down at the water.

"This ship really moves," said Michael.

"I wonder where the steering wheel is?" asked Luke.

"You have to go to the bridge," interrupted the bartender. "How are you gents today?"

"Great!" answered Johnny. "We are just exploring the ship. It's so huge."

"I'm James," he said pointing to his nametag. "Can I get you a soda or something?"

All three of the boys nodded and walked over to the bar.

"If you boys would like to see the bridge, there is a walkway right over there where you can see down into it," said James.

"Can we go in it?" asked Luke as they looked down.

"I don't think so. I think only special guests of the Captain are allowed to see it," James answered.

"Let's go see another deck," suggested Johnny.

"See ya, James," the boys yelled as they ran out the doorway.

The boys walked outside and down some steps toward the back of the boat. All of a sudden Johnny stopped and pointed.

"There it is!" he exclaimed. "The sports deck! And it looks awesome!"

The boys ran as fast as they could without spilling their drinks and found a small crowd of kids who seemed to be exploring also. A basketball game was going on in the middle of the sports deck.

"I wonder if they ever lose a basketball?" asked Michael.

"The net around the court is pretty high," noted Johnny.

"Hey, look over there. A putt-putt golf course and an in-line skating area," said Luke.

"I've got a feeling we're going to spend a lot of time here," said Johnny as he was reading a bulletin board. "It says here that they have dodgeball, volley-ball, and basketball tournaments up here."

"Hey, look over there. There's even a rock climbing wall," said Luke.

Michael walked over to the board and ran his finger down the notice.

"Tomorrow, open basketball, 2 p.m." he said. "I think that's for us.

"How about we go explore one more deck and then get ready for dinner," suggested Johnny.

The boys made it to the elevator and decided to go to Deck 3. It was full of staterooms just like Deck 2. Some of the rooms faced inward and some faced the water. At the far end of Deck 3 was a small movie theatre.

"I hope they have popcorn," said Luke.

Johnny looked at the listing of the movies to be played that week.

"No Bond!" he laughed.

The mention of James Bond threw them into a fit of pretending to shoot each other. They were laughing and carrying on when a couple of men with white jumpsuit uniforms came hurrying toward them down

221

the hall. The boys initially thought that the men were coming to talk to them, but the men ran past them without a glance.

"I wonder what's going on?" asked Johnny.

"Let's follow them," said Luke.

The boys ran up the stairs behind the men, trying not to get too close.

"They are security for the ship," said Luke. "It says it on the backs of their uniforms."

The men slowed down when they came to the customer service desk on Deck 5. The boys didn't get too close, but were near enough to hear what was going on. The men were talking to someone behind the desk and to a couple who were very upset.

"They said someone broke into their room and stole their gold jewelry," repeated Johnny.

"And some money too," added Michael.

The woman started crying when she talked about how old some of her jewelry was.

"I hope they find the person who stole the stuff," said Luke. "Otherwise that couple isn't going to have a very fun trip."

"We'd better go change for dinner," suggested Johnny.

"Yeah, there's nothing we can do here," said Michael.

With that, the boys walked away, occasionally glancing back at the sad couple.

CHAPTER NINE

Dinner on the first night of the cruise was full of excitement. People were searching for their assigned tables and everyone was dressed casually. The Captain was seated at a large oval table in the center of the dining room. It was reserved for special guests. Each of the nights on the cruise had a different theme. Some nights were casual, one was Hawaiian, and one was formal.

"I'm gonna skip dinner on formal night," said Luke pretending to loosen a tie from his neck.

"Yeah, I hate dressing up," added Johnny. "My mom will take a thousand pictures that night. She loves her new digital camera."

The boys sat down. Their table was set for ten people. The boys introduced themselves to an older couple from Canada who were celebrating their forty year wedding anniversary. A mother and daughter from Texas were also at the table. They were celebrating the daughter's graduation from college. Johnny and Michael looked at Luke blush when they found out that the daughter's name was Mary Beth.

"Is there something wrong?" asked the new Mary Beth.

"No, I just know another person with the same name at home," answered Luke. "Luckily, you are a lot older than her."

The last person to come to the table was a tall man with blond hair parted to one side. He was likely in his mid-twenties. It was obvious to the boys that the new Mary Beth was attracted to his good looks.

"Good evening, everyone. My name is Hans," he said with a slight accent.

Hans told everyone at the table that he was originally from Germany and was traveling alone. Everyone at the table shared a little about themselves while Johnny's mom took pictures of the guests at the table and especially of the boys.

"C'mon Mom, knock it off," Johnny pleaded. "How many pictures are you going to take?"

"At least one more," Hans answered.

Hans was on Johnny's right and he leaned in toward Johnny and the other boys until the flash went off.

The waiter and assistant waiter arrived at the table and handed everyone a menu. They introduced themselves and explained that they were from Croatia, a small country in Europe. They suggested certain items on the elaborate menu and took orders from everyone.

"Are you boys all brothers?" asked Hans.

"You would think so," answered Johnny's mom with a laugh. "They are just very good friends."

"We do everything together," said Michael. "Baseball, football, basketball. Pretty much everything."

"I play basketball too," replied Hans.

"Two p.m. tomorrow. Open basketball on the sports deck," said Johnny.

"I'll be there," said Hans.

The waiters returned to the table and began to serve everyone's food. The boys quickly found out they could have seconds of anything they wanted. Michael ate three bowls of lobster bisque and two salads. Everyone had a nice time at dinner, and no one left hungry.

"I'm getting really tired," said Luke.

"I think I ate too much," replied Michael.

The three boys all agreed to head back to the room and get to bed early. They wanted to be rested for their first full day at sea.

CHAPTER TEN

"**G**ood morning, this is the captain speaking," Captain Olaf said over the speaker in the stateroom. "Today will be sunny and 85 degrees. We hope you have a wonderful day on the Emerald of the Seas."

The boys quickly put on their swim trunks and ran outside. Balde was near the cart that held the supplies he needed to take care of the staterooms.

"Good morning, young men," said Balde.

"Hi Balde," said Johnny.

Balde reached into his pocket and pulled out some more chocolate squares.

"Thanks!" said the boys.

Balde gave them a wink and the boys ran down the hall to the elevator.

The pool deck was full of people, and the boys looked around until they found Johnny's mom and dad sitting in a couple of deck chairs.

"Morning boys, had any breakfast yet?" asked Johnny's dad.

"I'm still stuffed from last night!" exclaimed Luke.

The boys ran off to the pool where they swam and played for most of the morning. They ate an early lunch in the buffet line at the back of the ship and then returned to sit in one of the hot tubs next to the pool.

"Hey, it's almost two o'clock," said Michael. "I say we go get an ice cream and then grab our basketball shoes."

In no time at all, the boys were on the sports deck waiting to join in the open basketball game. Hans was already there; he was put on the opposite team from the boys. The teams were made up of different aged players and seemed to be balanced fairly.

"Play to 21 and call your own fouls," said the crew member on the sports deck.

The game went back and forth, each team scoring easily on the other. The teenager who was covering Hans was having trouble keeping him from driving to the basket. Each team only needed one basket to end the game.

"Can we call a time out?" said Michael.

Both teams agreed to a short time out, and Michael called his team together.

"We have to stop Hans," said Michael. "I think we can do it."

"He's just like Doug Wright," said Johnny. "He always goes to his right."

The teenager nodded and the team went back to the court. Hans got the ball and quickly drove to his right and went right to the basket for an easy layup to end the game. Both teams congratulated each other and two new teams took the court.

"Oh well, can't win them all," said Luke. "How about some putt-putt?"

The boys played on the sports deck until just before dinner. They headed down to their stateroom to clean up and get ready.

As they came closer to their room, the boy saw more security officers talking to a man in the doorway of his stateroom. They continued on and ran into Balde just outside their own room.

"What's going on, Balde?" asked Johnny.

"The people in that room were robbed," he said. "That's all I know."

Luke told Balde the story of the people the boys had seen at the customer service desk.

"That's horrible," said Balde. "I can't believe someone would do this."

He reminded them that dinner time was approaching. Before the boys headed into the room, he handed them each another chocolate.

CHAPTER ELEVEN

Everyone in the dining room was dressed in Hawaiian shirts and flowered dresses. The waiters were dressed similarly and each wore a string of flowers called a lei around his neck. Everyone was seated at the same places as the night before. The boys were the last ones to sit at their table and quickly had to order dinner. Johnny turned to speak to Hans, who was seated on his right.

"Nice game, Hans," said Johnny.

"Huh?" replied Hans.

"The basketball game, nice game," repeated Johnny.

"Oh yeah, thank you," said Hans.

Johnny's mom got up and started taking pictures of everyone.

"Mom, don't you have enough pictures?" Johnny said.

"You can't have enough memories," said Johnny's mom.

"Someone was robbed on our floor today," Michael announced.

"And it's happened more than once already," added Luke.

The older couple from Canada seemed very interested in the robbery and continued to talk about it until the waiters returned with their food.

"Excuse me," said Hans as he bumped elbows with Johnny.

"No problem," replied Johnny. "I'll move over a bit."

During dinner a man with a ukulele played songs as he walked around the three-story dining room. Michael ate two of everything and even had three desserts.

"There is a show tonight," said Johnny's dad. "Dancers and singers, I heard."

The boys watched as the new Mary Beth gathered up her courage and asked Hans to go to the show with her. He agreed, and after dinner everyone walked down to the large auditorium and awaited the start of the show.

"Let's sit in the balcony," suggested Luke.

The balcony seating surrounded the entire auditorium and offered a nice view of the stage and the seats below.

"Look, there are my mom and dad sitting down there on the left," said Johnny.

"There are Mary Beth and Hans down front in the middle," said Michael as he pointed in their direction.

The music from a small orchestra began, and the cruise director walked out onto the stage. He started the show by telling a few cruise jokes and then introduced the dancers and singers. The hour-long show was a medley of music from the 1940's all the way to the present.

"I can't believe the dancers stay on their feet so well," whispered Michael, "with the ship rocking and swaying the way it does."

"Some of us are more coordinated than others," replied Johnny jokingly.

"Oh yeah, I'd like to see you try that with those high heels the girls are wearing," said Michael.

The show ended with a grand finale that made the crowd rise to its feet. After the entertainers finished taking their bows, Captain Olaf walked to the center of the stage.

"Ladies and gentlemen, it is not usually our policy to worry you unnecessarily, but I feel I must inform you of some unfortunate activity on the Emerald of the Seas," he said. "I regret to say that there have been a number of burglaries on our ship since it has set sail."

The crowd let out a slight gasp and the captain began to talk again.

"As a matter of fact, there was a burglary while we were all sitting here enjoying the show," Captain Olaf said. "I would ask you to lock all your valuables in the safes provided in the staterooms for your safety. The crew and the security team are working diligently on this matter and we vow to stop the crimes being committed. Thank you for your cooperation."

Johnny leaned over toward Michael and Luke.

"Take a good look around," he said.

"Why?" asked Luke.

"Because no one in this room committed the burglary that just happened," stated Johnny. "Everyone here has an alibi."

Michael and Luke stood up as people were beginning to leave the auditorium and tried to focus on who was there and, maybe more importantly, who was not.

CHAPTER TWELVE

The Emerald of the Seas arrived at the island owned by the Regal Crown Cruise line early in the morning. Sunshine Bay was a small island that the cruise line had purchased over ten years before and turned into a private retreat only accessible to the guests of the cruise ship. The boys hurried through the buffet breakfast line and met Johnny's parents on Deck 1. This lower deck was used to move guests on and off the ship.

"Oh cool, we get to take a ferry boat to the island," said Luke.

"It's actually called a tender," corrected Johnny's dad.

The boys loaded onto the tender and quickly ran to the top level to sit in the sun. The ride was short and quite smooth. Sunshine Bay was designed like a small town with shops and places to get something to drink. The boys put their towels down on some chairs by the beach overlooking a swimming area.

"We're gonna go look around," yelled Johnny to his mom as they took off down the beach.

The island was a lot larger than the boys originally thought. It had multiple swimming beaches and even an area designed specifically for snorkeling. The boys ran further down the beach and found what they were looking for.

"There it is!" exclaimed Luke. "It's huge."

"It's definitely the biggest one I've ever seen!" added Johnny.

"Let's go sign up," said Michael.

There was already a fairly large group waiting to get into the trampoline and aqua park. The water trampoline could hold at least ten kids at one time. It was in the center of the park area, surrounded by a number of floating air-filled climbing structures and even a slide. In the shallower part of the park kids were aiming water guns at each other. A huge mountain-like peak at the back of the park was named Everest. It was obviously very difficult to climb and the boys noted that no one was even half-way up it.

"It's got to be fifty feet high," said Johnny.

"It doesn't look like it's easy to get a grip on it," noted Michael. "Plus anytime more than one person is on it, the whole thing shakes."

"There he goes," Luke said as he pointed to some-one falling to the water.

A bell rang, indicating that it was time for another group of people to enter the park. The crew members limited the time you could stay in the park to avoid crowding. The boys immediately ran for the water guns and after sufficiently drenching each other raced to the trampoline.

"Back flip," yelled Johnny. "Try a back flip."

Luke flipped around easily and landed on his feet. Michael tried to follow, made it around to his knees, and was shot off the trampoline into the water. Luke and Johnny leaned over the edge to lift Michael back up when he pulled the two of them into the water.

"Let's go climb Everest," he said.

Johnny, Luke and Michael all swam to the base, grabbed at the grips, and started climbing the side of the air-filled mountain. At one point someone on the other side crashed down and bounced off into the water. The impact of the shift in air pressure almost shot Johnny into the air.

"Hold on, Johnny!" screamed Michael.

The boys continued to climb slowly, avoiding the shifts in position and maintaining their balance.

"This is tiring," said Luke.

"Not too much farther," encouraged Johnny.

People on the shore were pointing to the boys, noting that they were close to the top.

"I made it!" exclaimed Johnny.

"Me too," added Michael.

Luke finished his climb and clutched the hand-hold at the top of the mountain.

"I'm on top of the world!" Luke screamed as he stood up.

Unexpectedly the mountain shifted a few feet to one side and all three boys fell backwards into the water. The boys surfaced, laughing at the fall, and noticed people cheering from shore. Michael was just about to suggest they climb it again when the bell rang to indicate that their session was done.

"Let's go to the volleyball court," said Johnny.

"Maybe we can play," said Luke.

The boys ran across to the other side of the island where the sand volleyball court was located. Two large bleachers were beside it.

"There is already a tournament going on," said Michael.

"Let's go watch for awhile," said Johnny.

Luke ran up to the top of the bleachers and the other two boys followed and sat down next to him.

"Whoa, did you see that?" pointed out Johnny.

Hans was on the left side of the front row of his team. The player in the middle had just set the ball to him and he slammed the ball downward with his left hand over the blockers on the other team.

"I sure did. That was impressive," said Michael.

Hans hit three more left handed smashes for a total of four consecutive points in a row. His team had won the game. Everyone on both sides seemed to enjoying themselves. Little did they know that back on the ship another burglary was being committed right at that very moment.

CHAPTER THIRTEEN

The ship sailed all night and arrived at the Caribbean island just as the sun was rising. Many of the guests had scheduled excursions that ranged from snorkeling to parasailing. Johnny, Michael, and Luke had decided to go shopping with Johnny's parents and then go on a zip line tour. It was evident that a lot of the people who like to cruise also like to shop. The downtown area of the island was bustling with shoppers buying clothing, souvenirs, and jewelry. For the boys, the shopping couldn't have been more boring.

"Let's go back to the ship and wait for our excursion," said Johnny's dad.

"Finally!" replied Johnny.

A small man near the ship was holding up a sign that said Canopy Tours.

"There it is. There's our tour," said Luke.

After everyone checked in, the tour operator announced that they were ready to go. They all piled into a large open air bus for the half hour ride to the mountainous area where the excursion started. When they arrived, the instructor asked everyone to circle around him.

"Safety is of extreme importance here at Canopy Tours," said the instructor. "You will be riding on a zip line from platform to platform across the mountainous forest."

The instructor showed the boys how to attach their climbing gear and check it for tightness. Once the harness was in place, the boys started the climb the stairs to the platform.

"Wow, this is getting pretty high up here," said Michael.

"We need to get pretty far up to start," replied Johnny. "Then gravity will move us down the zip line to the next platform."

The boys reached the platform high in the air. Above them was the first wire zip line.

"It's a long way down," said Michael as his voice cracked.

"Are you scared of heights, Michael?" asked Luke.

"No!" he said quickly.

Michael's face started to turn a little white and he grabbed the railing of the platform.

"I mean yes!" he exclaimed.

The instructor helped Michael to the center of the platform and connected his harness to the zip line. Michael reached up slowly and grabbed the two handles above him.

"Best way to get over your fear is to just go and go quickly," prodded the instructor.

Michael walked to the edge and took a deep breath. He backed up a couple of inches and then launched forward off the platform.

"Wahooooo!" he yelled as he slid down the zip line. Johnny and Luke cheered until Michael reached the other platform far in the distance.

Luke and Johnny followed behind, screaming all the way down.

"I think there are twenty more!" said Michael. "I'll go first again."

Michael flew off toward the next platform that was located in the dense part of the forest.

"I guess he's not afraid of heights anymore," noted Johnny.

The Canopy Tour took the boys down the mountain through valleys and even over a waterfall. After the excursion, the boys returned to the ship walked down the hall on Deck 9.

"That was the coolest thing I've ever done," said Michael.

"I didn't think you were even going to go at first," said Luke.

"Yeah, your face was as white as a ghost!" said Johnny.

As the boys walked up to their room, they noticed someone different working at the cart that held the stateroom supplies.

"Hey, where's Balde?" asked Johnny.

"I have some bad news," replied the new cabin steward. "They have confined him to his quarters with a guard outside."

"Why?" asked Michael.

"Well, they suspect he has been behind the thefts the last few days," said the steward.

"No!" exclaimed Johnny. "It can't be. Balde would never do something like that."

The cabin steward agreed. He told the boys that they had not found any of the missing items, but some guests had noted that Balde was often seen in the vicinity of some of the rooms that were burglarized.

"Don't let it concern you," said the steward. "You are on vacation."

The boys entered the room and plopped down on the bed. They were depressed about the accusations surrounding their new friend.

"We have to find out who really did this," said Johnny.

"And soon," added Luke.

CHAPTER FOURTEEN

The next day the ship stopped at another island. The boys wanted to stay on the ship to search for anything that would help Balde, but Johnny's mom and dad made them go to the beach. Johnny's dad insisted that there was nothing they could do, but the boys, of course, thought otherwise. After a long day of swimming and snorkeling, they all returned to the ship to find that the robberies had stopped.

The boys were happy that the cruise ship would be at sea the whole next day. Morning came fast and the boys started the day by roaming the halls of the ship looking for anything or anyone suspicious. At lunch-time they met at the buffet at the back of the ship.

"Find anything?" asked Luke.

"Not a thing," said Michael. "I saw very few people all morning."

"We won't be on this ship much longer," noted Johnny. "If we don't figure out who the robber is soon, Balde will be blamed for something that I'm sure he didn't do."

The boys decided to take a break from roaming the halls and play open basketball again on the sports deck. As they got up to leave, they noticed Hans sitting a few tables away.

"Hi Hans. Nice spikes!" said Michael.

Hans looked a little confused and grabbed at his hair.

"Spikes?" he replied.

"Yeah, those left handed smashes on the volleyball court," said Johnny.

"Oh those," said Hans. "Uh, thank you."

"Are you going to open basketball, Hans?" asked Luke. "We are heading there right after we get our basketball shoes."

"I think so," said Hans.

The boys took off and raced to their room. In just a few moments, they were out the door and on the elevator.

When they arrived at the sports deck, Hans was already there.

"How did you get here so quickly?" asked Luke.

"I guess I'm just fast," Hans immediately replied.

Again, they were placed on a team opposite Hans, but this time they had a couple of really good players on their side. Before the game started, Michael told the player who was going to guard Hans that he always drove to his right.

"To his right," Michael said again.

"Yeah, that's why we lost the last game," added Luke. "He kept driving to his strong side."

The game got underway and the player guarding Hans was definitely overplaying him, trying to make him dribble with his left hand. Hans effortlessly drove to the left and left the player a little confused.

"I thought you said he goes to his right?" said the player to Michael.

The other team scored quickly and the game was over in a very short time. Hans had continued driving to the left and easily made his left-handed layups. The boys left the basketball court and went to their stateroom.

"I don't get it," said Michael. "We couldn't stop him."

"Last time he played he moved like Doug Wright," said Luke. "Oh well, can't win them all."

CHAPTER FIFTEEN

The pool looked inviting after the hot game of basketball. The deck was filled with swimmers and lots of others listening to the band. The boys cooled off in the pool, showing off their best cannonballs. The cruise director grabbed the microphone when the music stopped and informed everyone on the pool deck that tonight would be international night and also formal night. He said that Regal Crown Cruise line was very proud of the fact that many of the guests came from many different nations. He also said that his crew came from over forty different countries.

"We have a special promotion going on today," the cruise director said. "In honor of our international night, if you can get twenty-five names of people from twenty-five different countries on a sheet of paper, we will give you a Regal Crown T-shirt. First names and country is all we require."

The boys jumped out of the pool and each grabbed a paper and pencil and started to collect names. Most of the kids on the deck were scrambling for names by asking people where they were from. The boys got a few names and then ran over to Richard.

"Hello cruise boys, I suppose you need me to sign your paper," he said. "There you go. Richard and Jamaica."

"You sure wear a lot of necklaces," noted Luke.

"Yeah, once I get a new one I just add it to the collection," answered Richard. "Makes me feel good, too."

Johnny spotted Hans and ran over to get his signature.

"Can you sign your name and country?" asked Johnny.

Hans grabbed the pen with his left hand and wrote his name on the paper.

"Hans. Germany," read Johnny out loud. "Thanks."

The boys only needed a few signatures and decided to go to other decks to see if they could find some people from other countries.

The boys ran down to Deck 9 and found only two more signatures for their list. They jumped down a few flights of stairs to Deck 7 and ran into Hans. Johnny stopped in front of him and looked at him for a second or two. Hans had changed clothes and his hair was parted to the side. Johnny flipped over his piece of paper and held up his pen.

"Hans, we are collecting names for a contest," Johnny said.

"Johnny, we already got.....," Luke spit out as he was elbowed in the ribs.

"No, Luke," Johnny interrupted. "We still need one more name for our list."

"Just your first name and the country you are from," Michael added.

Hans grabbed the pen with his right hand and signed his name followed by his home country of Germany.

The boys continued walking down the hall until they were out of sight and then Johnny started to run.

"What was that all about?" said Luke rubbing his side.

"I'll tell you when we get to the room," said Johnny.

CHAPTER SIXTEEN

"Why were you acting so weird back there?" asked Luke.

"I know who has been stealing from the state-rooms!" exclaimed Johnny.

"How do you know?" asked Michael.

"Well, remember when Officer Bill came to our class last week? He said we had to use the power of observation," said Johnny. "Up until now we weren't being very observant."

Johnny got up off the bed and ran into his mom and dad's adjoining room. He returned to their room with his mom's new digital camera.

"There is a picture of the burglar on my mom's camera!" pointed out Johnny.

After he spent a few minutes explaining his theory, the boys all agreed that they had solved the mystery.

"How are we gonna prove it?" asked Michael.

"Well, I think the best way will be to catch them in the act," said Johnny.

"Not necessarily," stated Luke.

Luke got off the bed and stood up. He laid out a plan that all three agreed could work.

"We definitely will need the walkie talkies," Luke stated.

"We need a code word to start the whole thing in motion," said Michael.

"I think we should call it Knuckles," said Johnny.

"Yeah, Operation Knuckles!" exclaimed Luke.

There was a knock on the door and Johnny's mom walked in. She was carrying a bunch of plastic-covered clothes on hangers.

"I have your clothes for tonight here," said Johnny's mom. "We rented tuxedos for you boys."

"Tuxedos?" questioned Michael.

"Oh no!" Luke groaned.

"Mom!" Johnny whined.

"I don't want to hear any more out of you three," she said. "Now start getting ready for dinner and get those tuxedos on."

CHAPTER SEVENTEEN

Johnny left the room first and began to search the ship. He was dressed in his black tuxedo and his basketball shoes, knowing that he would have to run fast. Luke and Michael took their time and left the room just before dinner.

"Any sign of him yet?" Luke said over his walkie talkie.

"Not yet," replied Johnny. "I'll keep looking and report back."

"Only code words from now on," said Luke.

"Don't worry, I'll find him," said Johnny.

Luke and Michael walked slowly, trying to delay their entrance to the dining room. The boys finally arrived at the table and sat down with the rest of the group. Everyone else at the table was already seated including the older couple, the new Mary Beth and her mother, Johnny's parents, and Hans.

"Where's Johnny?" asked his mom.

"Umm, he was still in the shower when we left," lied Michael.

"He said he'd be here soon," added Luke.

International night was definitely a big affair for everyone in the dining room. The waiters were dressed up more than usual and they offered a menu made of dishes from many different countries.

Luke and Michael were getting nervous waiting for Johnny to call when the walkie talkie crackled.

"Knuckles, Operation Knuckles," said Johnny.

Luke quickly stood up and asked to be excused. Instead of waiting for an answer, he darted off and out of sight.

"Where is he going?" asked Johnny's dad.

"Restroom, I think," Michael fibbed.

Johnny was hiding behind a corner off one of the halls of Deck 3. A man down the hall was standing in front of one of the staterooms, fidgeting with some sort of electronic device. The man looked to his right and left, and the door finally opened.

"I don't think you should go in there," said Johnny. "And I bet that's not your room."

Luke looped back into the dining room and approached the large oval table where Captain Olaf was seated.

"Captain, sir, I believe there is something you should know," said Luke calmly. "There has been another burglary. And the man whose room was robbed is sitting at my table. I thought you should tell him."

"Show me to your table, young man," the captain said. "We'll tell him right away."

The captain stood and asked the guests at his table to excuse him. He motioned to one of his assistants and asked him to find security and bring them to him immediately.

The man on Deck 3 froze and gave Johnny a frightening stare. Just as Luke had planned, the man started to run after Johnny. Since Johnny was the fastest boy in his grade, he hoped he could stay in front of the man without being caught. Running in a tuxedo didn't help, but having basketball shoes on sure did.

Luke walked with Captain Olaf toward their dining table and pointed out Hans on the way over. When they arrived, Captain Olaf cleared his throat.

"I regret to inform you, sir, that your room has been robbed," the captain said.

A few security men arrived and stood directly behind the captain.

"I don't see how . . . I mean . . . but that's impossible," stuttered Hans.

"Why don't you accompany us to your room and we will sort this out," said Captain Olaf.

The captain asked Hans his room number as they left the table and walked out of the dining room.

Johnny was running as fast as he could toward the end of deck 3. The man wasn't that close, but with his longer legs he was gaining on Johnny.

"Michael!" Johnny yelled into his walkie talkie. "Deck 5, starboard, moving forward."

Michael jumped up as he got his cue. Johnny's mom and dad tried to ask what was going on but Michael was gone before they could utter any words.

"I don't understand what is going on here," said Hans. "This must be some sort of mistake."

Captain Olaf, Luke, and the security men followed Hans, who complained about the interruption to his dinner all the way to his room on Deck 7. When they arrived, Hans quickly opened the door and looked inside.

"See? Nothing is wrong here. Nothing at all," said Hans.

He pulled the door shut and stood out in the hall.

Michael found the cart that Johnny had stashed in the middle of deck 5. He arrived just in time to watch Johnny come running down the hall. Michael peeked around the corner and saw the man trailing just behind Johnny. Just as Johnny passed him, Michael gave the cart a hard shove into the hall and the man crashed into it, knocking it over and falling to the floor himself. Michael took off toward the elevator and closed the door.

"Deck 7, Johnny," said Michael into his walkie talkie.

The man picked himself off the floor as Johnny heard Michael's instructions. Johnny turned to see the man running again and he headed up the stairs toward deck 7.

"I don't understand why my dinner was interrupted with this false information," said Hans. "Who told you this, anyway?"

The captain turned toward Luke and was about to answer when Johnny came flying by, stopping just past the security men. To everyone's surprise, a man came running around the corner and stopped abruptly when he saw them. A man who looked, except for his clothing, exactly like Hans!

"I think you will find that only one of these men is registered aboard your boat, Captain Olaf," Johnny gasped. "The other must have stowed away somehow."

"One would commit the burglaries and the other act normally on the ship," said Michael as he walked up.

"Then they would switch places and the other one would do the crimes," added Luke.

The captain ordered the security men to hold Hans and his twin brother while they searched their room more completely. They found a suitcase full of stolen jewelry and money under the bed.

"Take these criminals down to the cell and lock them up," said Captain Olaf to the security men.

"You meddling kids, if it wasn't for you we would have gotten away with this," said the twin as he was escorted away.

CHAPTER EIGHTEEN

The captain was seated next to Johnny at the table, telling everyone the details of the twins' capture.

"I still don't get how you knew that Hans had a twin," said Johnny's dad.

"The power of observation, Dad," said Johnny. "At first I didn't notice because I wasn't being very observant, but as I had more clues it started to make sense."

"Like what?" asked the new Mary Beth.

"Well, the first time we played basketball he always drove to his right," Michael jumped in. "And the next time we played he always went to the left."

"He sat on my right side at dinner. The first night we never bumped into each other at all. The next night he bumped my elbow each time we tried to eat," said Johnny.

"Then there was the time we watched Hans spike the ball four times in a row with his left hand," added Luke. "When we complemented him, he didn't even remember it!"

"I still don't see how you figured it out with only that information," questioned Captain Olaf.

"We finally figured it out when we were getting our signatures for the free t-shirt for international night. I asked Hans to sign his name and he did it with his left hand," said Johnny.

"Then we saw him a couple of minutes later on a different floor. He was dressed completely different and signed our sheet with his right hand," Luke said.

"Yeah, no one does that," stated Michael.

"I hate to admit this but you helped us figure it out too, Mom!" said Johnny reluctantly. "I bet you never noticed that the twins parted their hair on different sides."

Johnny's mom looked a little puzzled.

"We looked at the pictures on your digital camera that you took from different nights at dinner," said Luke.

"I bet you won't mind me taking pictures in the future," she said proudly.

"They aren't just twins, you see; they are mirror twins," said Johnny. "Even though they look alike, they mirror each other. One is right handed and one is left handed."

"We learned all about different kind of twins from Mrs. G," added Michael. "She has twins of her own."

"Fascinating," said the captain.

Captain Olaf raised his glass in the air and pointed it at Johnny's mom and dad.

"You brought some mighty fine boys along with you on this cruise," he said. "And the Regal Crown Cruise line is in your debt."

Everyone toasted their glasses to each other and the boys were about to take a drink when a hand touched each one of them on the shoulder.

"Balde!" the boys cried out.

The boys jumped up and each gave Balde a hug. Balde was obviously grateful and thanked them for what they had done.

"By the way, have you boys ever been on the bridge of a cruise ship?" the captain asked.

"This is the best vacation ever," Luke exclaimed. "I think I want to live here!"

Johnny, Luke, and Michael made their fists as they always did and touched them together. Just then Balde and the Captain also made their hands into fists and touched them to the boys.

"Knuckles!" the boys yelled, smiling from ear to ear.

The captain turned to Balde and put his arm around his shoulder.

"The boys tell me you make some amazing animals with towels," said Captain Olaf.

Captain Olaf winked at the boys. Everything had turned out just fine.